NAME GOES HERE

Hiccup and his pet dragon, Toothless

ABOUT THE AUTHOR

Hiccup Horrendous Haddock the Third was destined
to be the next Chief of the Hairy Hooligan Tribe, and
the greatest Viking Hero who ever lived.

But Hiccup's memoirs look back to when he was a
very ordinary boy and it looked like destiny might have
made some sort of MISTAKE. In this volume, Hiccup
has to steal the antidote to Vorpentitis from a madman
with an axe, and return back to Berk before the
Doomfang catches him.

I dedicate this book to JOSHUA

Little, Brown and Company

Hachette Book Group USA
1271 Avenue of the Americas, New York, NY 10020
Visit our Web site at www.lb-kids.com

First U.S. Edition: April 2007
First published in Great Britain in 2006 by Hodder Children's Books
The characters and events portrayed in this book are fictitious. Any similarity to real persons, living or dead, is coincidental and not intended by the author.

ISBN-10: 0-316-11425-1
ISBN-13: 978-0-316-11425-7

10 9 8 7 6 5 4 3 2 1

RRD-C

Printed in the United States of America

please note: Some people say that THERE IS NO SUCH THING AS DRAGONS. But what I want to know is – have these people actually ever BEEN to the Dark Ages?

How to Cheat ~a~ Dragon's Curse

The Heroic Misadventures of

Hiccup Horrendous Haddock III

as told to

CRESSIDA COWELL

LITTLE, BROWN AND COMPANY

New York ·ɔ· Boston

Map of
BARBARI
during the worst w
THE SULLEN S
has frozen over
MOUNT VILLAINY
is good for skiing
THE DOOMFANG is trapped under the ice
in THE WRATH OF THOR
Beware of the Hysterical Tribe
who live here on HYSTERIA
(they're completely CRAZY)

e
RCHIPELAGO
for 100 years

THE
ISLE
OF
BERK
is deep in snow

Will this winter
NEVER end?

Will the spring
NEVER come?

~ CONTENTS ~

stoick
the
Vast

...micazi
(...rglar and
...word fighter)

Clueless

Fishlegs

Norbert
the
NUTJOB
(completely crazy
chief)

I am the Venomous Vorpent
And my sting is as deadly as a Black Widow spider.
Even before this story begins
I have already stung one of the characters.
(I hope he is not your favorite)
And although he does not know it yet
THE CURSE IS COME UPON HIM!

My poison is creeping through his body,
My strong venom is killing his heart.
And at ten o'clock on Friday morning
He shall DIE as sure as fish eggs are fish eggs.
Because NOBODY can CHEAT
THE CURSE of the VENOMOUS VORPENT.

1. THE HUNTING-WITH-BOWS-AND-ARROWS-ON-SKIS EXPEDITION

Winters were always cold in the Viking Lands.

But this winter was the coldest in a hundred years. It was *so* cold that the Sullen Sea had frozen over, and all the islands in the Inner Isles were now joined together by a great flat desert of solid ice, two meters thick in places.

On this particularly cold morning several hours before breakfast, it was as if the whole world was holding

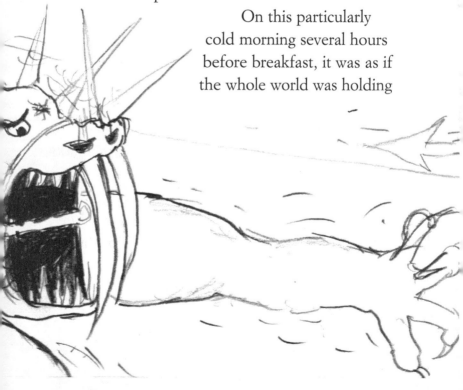

its breath, frozen in time. The air was as sharp as broken glass; no sound disturbed the pure snowy silence.

No sound, that is, apart from an appalling, mad screaming coming from somewhere out in the middle of the ice.

For a small party of young boys and their teacher from the Hooligan Tribe had set out from the little Isle of Berk where they lived to the Island of Villainy to the south.

Not in a *boat*, of course, for you cannot sail across a frozen sea.

They were speeding far too fast across the ice in an enormous wooden Viking SLEIGH, pulled by six pure white Saber-Toothed Driver Dragons larger than lions and faster than cheetahs.

The dreadful mad yelling was coming from the man driving the sleigh, Gobber the Belch. Gobber was the teacher in charge of the Pirate Training Program on Berk, and he was an enormous monster of a man wrapped up in furs who could easily have been mistaken for a grizzly bear with a dirty red beard and an attitude problem.

"GEDDONWITHIT, YOU MISERABLE WHITE *WORMS!*" roared Gobber at the Saber-Toothed Dragons, cracking his whip above their heads. "I'VE HAD SNAILS THAT HAVE MOVED QUICKER THAN YOU LOT! MY GRANNY COULD SKIP FASTER THAN THIS AND SHE'S A HUNDRED AND FOUR! YEEEEEEHAAH!!"

One gigantic furry arm lashed out with a whip that curled through the air like a great black serpent, the other shook the reins in a lunatic frenzy that sent

the Driver Dragons bounding forward in terrible uncontrolled leaps.

Behind Gobber on the sleigh sat twelve of his pupils.

Ten of these boys were ugly young thugs yelling as loudly in crazy excitement as their teacher.

"YEEEEEEEHAAAAH!" they whooped, as the sleigh hit a snowbank and sailed ten meters through the air and then slammed back down on the ice with stomach-churning violence.

"YEEEEEEEEEEEEEEEEEHAAAAAAH!!"

The last two boys were smaller than the rest and a lot less excited.

"I'm glad," gasped Hiccup Horrendous Haddock the Third as the sleigh tipped over wildly on one runner with an awful screech and spray of ice. "I'm glad I didn't have breakfast because I think it would have come up again . . ."

Hiccup is, in fact, the Hero of this story, although you would never have guessed it to look at him. He was small, and red-haired, and very, very ordinary.

Hiccup's best friend Fishlegs, a skinny runner-bean of a boy with asthma and a squint, wasn't really listening. He was praying to Thor with his eyes squeezed tightly shut.

"Please, Thor," begged Fishlegs, "please make it stop . . ."

Fishlegs's prayer was about to be answered.

The sleigh was approaching the great black cliffs of the Visithugs Territories far too impossibly fast for it to stop in time . . .

"Don't open your eyes, Fishlegs," advised Hiccup.

Gobber the Belch reared up and with a mighty roar of "WOOOOOOAH!!!," leaned back so far pulling on the reins that he was nearly horizontal. The Saber-Tooths came to a plunging halt so sharply that the sleigh wheeled around in a mad arc. . . . They were going to slam into that cliff at such a speed they would all be smashed to splinters . . .

"AAAAARGH!" yelled Hiccup, shutting his eyes too.

The sleigh screeched to a quivering halt. Hiccup opened his eyes again. Astonishingly, they were still alive. But the smooth black wall of the cliff was only centimeters away from Hiccup's cheek. Hiccup held on to the rock for a second to help himself stop shaking.

"RIGHT!" bellowed Gobber, clambering out of the sleigh entirely unconcerned. "WHAT ARE YOU ALL DOING SKULKING IN THERE? GET OUT AND STAND TO ATTENTION, YOU PATHETIC DRIBBLES OF EARWIG DROPPINGS!"

Yawning and chattering, all twelve boys unpacked skis from the back of the sleigh and attached them to the bottom of their furry boots.

For six months of the year the Vikings lived

under SNOW . . . so a Viking Warrior had to be just as good at SKIING as he was at SAILING.

This was a Hunting-with-Bows-and-Arrows-on-Skis Expedition. The boys had to ski down Mount Villainy, the largest mountain in the Inner Isles, shooting with their arrows as many Semi-Spotted Snowpeckers as they could.

"I'm going to get at least FIFTY," boasted Snotface Snotlout, a tall thug of a boy with huge nostrils and a moustache like a little furry caterpillar squirming on his upper lip.

"SILENCE!" screamed Gobber, cracking his whip.

There was absolute silence immediately. It's a curious fact, but a heavily armed, mad, six-and-a-half-foot teacher holding a whip *tends* to get his class's attention.

"*I* will be staying here to guard the sleigh," yelled Gobber. "Hiccup Horrendous Haddock the Third will be in charge of the Hunting Party when you get to the mountain."

Ten of the boys groaned and turned around to look furiously at Hiccup.

ALL of them reckoned they would make better leaders than Hiccup.

Snotlout had won the Senseless Violence Cup three years in a row. Wartihog could smash chairs to pieces with his bare fists. Dogsbreath the Duhbrain burped so loud he shattered glass.

Small, skinny, and unimportant, only Hiccup looked like he had no leadership skills whatsoever. He stood on one leg apologetically and this made his skis cross and he fell over.

"Why does HICCUP get to be in charge AGAIN?" demanded Snotface Snotlout through gritted teeth.

"Because Hiccup is the son of the CHIEF and *one day* he will be in charge PERMANENTLY, Thor help us all . . . ," explained Gobber, helping Hiccup to his feet and dusting the snow off him with one hairy hand.

"Any questions?" boomed Gobber.

A rare picture of
↙ a Viking ski

Fishlegs put up his hand. "Just a *small* point, sir," he said. "How are we going to climb *up* the mountain in the first place?"

"The Saber-Toothed Dragons will DRAG you to the top ON your skis," replied Gobber. "It shouldn't take more than half an hour."

Fishlegs and Hiccup looked dubiously at the great white creatures crouching dangerously on the

Tuffnut Junior ↙

clueless ↓

DOGSbrea' the Duhbrain ↙

ice, tongues spilling out over teeth as sharp as swords, cat-like eyes gazing at their small human Masters with the purest hatred.

"So that's that, then," said Gobber. "I shall wait for you here and see you all in three hours' time. . . . I really need a NAP . . . way too early for me . . ."

Gobber settled himself on the furs of the sleigh and gave an enormous yawn. "Oh, and one more

Snotlout

Hiccu[

thing . . . as you know, nobody lives on the Island of Villainy, but the Island of Hysteria is just next door and I should warn you that at this time of year there *may* be Hysterics about . . ."

"HYSTERICS???" squeaked Fishlegs, somewhat, well, *hysterically.* "But the Hysterics are trapped safely in Hysteria, aren't they?"

HYSTERICS, I should explain, were a particularly bloodthirsty and lunatic Tribe of Vikings. Even tough Tribes like the Visithugs were scared of the Hysterics. Hiccup had never actually *met* a Hysteric, but he knew they were renowned for killing you first, and asking questions later.

Normally they didn't trouble the other Tribes, however, because three-quarters of the island ended in dizzyingly high cliffs plunging straight into deep seas, and on the north coast was the Wrath of Thor, where an impossibly huge and monstrous Sea Dragon called the DOOMFANG lived.

A page from one of Hiccup's notebooks from when he was much younger →

Dragon Hibernation

Most dragons hibernate in the winter. Big ones go in a cave but smaller ones dig themselves a hole to sleep in, and the deeper the hole, the colder the winter will be.

← A Common-or-Garden dragon hibernating for the winter.

Some dragons, like Saber-Toothed Driver Dragons, do not hibernate at all, and they are called evergreens, and this is a funny name for them because Saber-Toothed Driver Dragons are always white.

The good news about this was that nobody could get into Hysteria, and even more importantly, the Hysterics could not get out.

Except at this time of year . . .

"Because at *this* time of year," boomed Gobber happily, "the Wrath of Thor is all frozen over, and the Doomfang is trapped under two meters solid of ice. So if you *do* happen to come across a Hysteric — and I'm SURE you won't; it's far too early in the morning — I suggest you ski like fury in the opposite direction."

And just like that, Gobber fell asleep.

Saber-Toothed Driver Dragons

Saber-Tooths are enormous lionlike dragons that do not hibernate, and are therefore very useful to the Vikings for pulling their sleighs, and dragging them up mountains during the winter. They have been known to eat their owners.

I don't like happy endings. They are too neat, too nice. I like a little spice in my stories. So ...

~STATISTICS~

COLORS: Always white

ARMED WITH: Those terrible Saber-Teeth and super-scary spikes on head... 9

HUNTING ABILITY: Terrifying to watch... 9

SPEED: Not as quick as some, and their heavy bulk makes them slow to maneuver... 6

FEAR AND FIGHT FACTOR: Alarming... 9

2. SABER-TOOTHED DRIVER DRAGONS

Gobber's enormous snores rang out like a walrus calling out to another walrus some fifty icebergs away.

As if they were all a part of the same creature, the pack of Saber-Toothed Driver Dragons settled themselves down on the ice and refused to move. By Woden's Armpit, but those Drivers were BIG.

The boys looked at them.

"Well come on, then, Hiccup," grunted Wartihog impatiently. "Take charge!"

Hiccup cleared his throat and used his most reasonable voice. "OK, guys," he said in Dragonese.* "I don't want any trouble . . ."

"Oh look, it talksssss . . . ," hissed a particularly large and savage-looking Saber-Tooth. He was missing an eye, and from the specially royal way he held himself, seemed to be the Leader of the Pack. "The little Human Tadpole is speaking the noble Dragon tongue . . ."

The other Drivers laughed jeeringly.

*Dragonese was the language dragons spoke to each other. Only Hiccup understood this fascinating language.

Dogsbreath the Duhbrain and Snotface Snotlout

"We all know what we're supposed to be doing here . . . ," Hiccup continued.

"We know what WE'RE going to be doing," sneered the Driver, closing his one eye and settling himself comfortably. "We're going to have a nice long sleep right here while you sweat it up the largest mountain in the Inner Isles . . ."

"Oh for Thor's sake!" exploded Snotface Snotlout. "That girly 'speaking Dragonese' stuff isn't going to work with these brutes!"

Snotlout grabbed the black whip from Gobber's relaxed hand, and cracked it.

Snnnnnnaaaap!

The Driver Dragons blinked open their eyes.

Snotlout cracked the whip again, this time letting the end of it lash the face of the Saber-Tooth with the One Eye. The Driver sprang to his feet with a yowl of pain and the rest of the pack followed him, furious but respectful. The boys cheered.

"That's the way to do it!" grinned Snotlout, whipping another of the dragons for the pure pleasure of it. The animal howled and Snotlout laughed. "Disobey ME, would you, you SNIVELING

CRAWLING PIECES OF FORKED-TONGUE RUBBISH! *This'll* learn you!"

"Don't do that, Snotlout," said Hiccup quietly. Hiccup didn't normally stand up to Snotlout, but he couldn't bear to see an animal as proud and dignified as a Saber-Toothed Driver made to dance about like a monkey.

Snotlout stopped what he was doing to turn on Hiccup.

"What's this?" sneered Snotlout. "Is Hiccup the Useless trying to tell Snotlout the HERO what to do? Face it, Hiccup, the snow will turn as blue as Gobber the Belch's nose before YOU become the Chief of the Hooligan Tribe."

Snotlout snapped the whip, and it curled cruelly forward at Hiccup, hitting him on the chest.

It would have been a very painful lash, if it hadn't been for the fact that sleeping down Hiccup's waistcoat was Hiccup's small, disobedient hunting dragon, Toothless.

The cutting edge of the whip hit Toothless on the hard, horny skin of his behind, and woke him out of his hibernation sleep.

Toothless climbed up out of Hiccup's collar, sat on his shoulder, and puffed out his neck in fury. "S-something hit T-t-toothless on the b-b-bottom! H-h-how can T-t-toothless s-s-sleep with things hitting him on the b-b-bottom!"

Ha!Ha!

"Why isn't your ridiculous pinprick of a hunting dragon hibernating like all the others?" blustered Snotlout.

"I was worried he was getting too cold," replied Hiccup, soothing Toothless by scratching him softly in between the horns. "He didn't dig himself a deep enough Hibernation Hole, and if a dragon gets too cold he can stay asleep for centuries. So I dug him up and I've been carrying him around with me to keep him warm."

"And now T-t-toothless woken up too EARLY!" raged Toothless. "Issa f-f-freezing!"

"What," scoffed Snotlout, "what is your pathetic pinprick of a dragon" (for Toothless was the smallest

HA!

hunting dragon anybody has
ever seen, before or since),
"*what* is your ridiculous
frogspawn of a reptile
wearing?"

Toothless was wearing a
fur coat.

Hiccup had made it in
a desperate attempt to keep
the little dragon warm.

"Oh this is too
good —hold me up,

Dogsbreath!" snorted Snotlout. "Hiccup has made his ickle teeny dwagon an ickle teeny furry DRESS!"

"Issa c-c-coat!" hissed Toothless. "Issa C-C-COAT!"

"A dragon in a dress!" squealed Snotlout.

"HA HA HA HA!" roared the boys. "A dragon in a dress!"

Even the Saber-Toothed Driver Dragons joined in.

"Oh my Claws and Jaws," drawled One Eye. "I do believe that is the smallest hunting dragon I have EVER seen dressed up in HUMAN WRAPPINGS! Has it no shame?"

Poor Toothless stood up very straight and stiff on Hiccup's shoulder. Beginning with his horns and spreading slowly downward, he turned a delicate shade of pink. He closed his jaws tightly and smoke rings blew out of his ears.

"Issa v-v-very stylish winter COAT," he said gruffly. "Yer all j-j-jealous."

Snotlout started barking out orders. "OK, we've wasted enough time here. . . . Everybody get themselves into pairs and grab on to the harness of one of these Saber-Toothed Brutes. . . . You two LOSERS."

He pointed at Hiccup and Fishlegs. "Can have the half-blind one."

"You don't like us humans much, do you, One Eye?" said Hiccup as he and Fishlegs shuffled themselves into position behind the enormous Saber-Tooth.

One Eye spat a great burst of fire into the snow. "Don't like you?" he hissed. "I LOATHE you with every drop of my pure green blood. . . . You Humans are treacherous, ignorant, greedy, and violent. I have been Leader of my Pack for forty years through good times and hard. What does Snotlout know about TRUE Leadership? He's just a pig with a whip in his hand. My fangs ACHE with my hatred. . . . My claws ITCH to scratch out every single Two-Legged, Mud-Bound, Jaw-Flapping Human on this entire planet . . ."

"Oh great," said Fishlegs nervously. "We have a Driver Dragon who HATES us. This morning just gets better and better . . ."

By the time they got going, with One Eye dragging them VERY SLOWLY up the gorge, and through a thick pine forest, there was no sign of the other boys.

The forest ended as suddenly as it had begun, and

on the final sheer climb to the top of Mount Villainy they did not pass a single tree. One Eye halted at the peak of Mount Villainy. A lone boulder marked the Highest Point. Hanging on firmly to this rock to prevent the wind, or the sheer dizzying pull of the abyss, from carrying him over the edge, Hiccup peered down the other side of the mountain into the Wrath of Thor. Normally, the sea and the Doomfang roared

and raged through that spiteful slit, whirlpooling and
spiralling and crashing into each other. Now the crack
was still and frozen as Death itself, and the only sign of
the Doomfang was a dreadful moaning that drummed
in the ears like a headache, and a dark shadow moving
slowly under the ice, like a gigantic cloud building up
before a thunderstorm.

"Let's get out of here as quickly as we
can," shivered Fishlegs. "There
are a lot of grim,
creepy places

in the Barbaric Archipelago, but THIS has got to be the GRIMMEST and the CREEPIEST."

I don't know whether YOU have ever tried Hunting-with-Bows-and-Arrows-on-Skis, but it is really quite a complicated skill. Skiing downhill itself is difficult enough, and then you have to concentrate on actually HITTING the pesky little Semi-Spotted Snowpeckers, not too easy because they flit about like hummingbirds.

On top of the basic difficulties of the sport, Fishlegs was the most appalling skier and a terrible shot. His bow whirled around like a windmill as he tried to keep his balance, and even if his hands had been as steady as a rock, a dreadful squint meant that his eyes were as crossed as his skis, and frankly, any chance of him hitting ANYTHING AT ALL would be a matter of pure fluke. He wobbled forward, knees bent as if sitting on the toilet, skis pointing inward in the snowplow position, and at the first hint of a little bump in the snow he fell over and his skis fell off.

Hiccup wasn't as bad as Fishlegs, but any sport is not just about skill, it is also about HEART. And Hiccup's heart wasn't really in this. He was secretly on

the side of the Semi-Spotted
Snowpeckers, charming little birds that
Hiccup often watched from his window.
They built themselves interesting little nests
like tiny igloos.

So after an hour and a half, despite the fact that
Semi-Spotted Snowpeckers were jumping all around
them like fleas on a cow's back, Hiccup and Fishlegs
had shot not a single bird.

"Bother, bother, bother!" exclaimed Hiccup as
he missed yet another one.

One Eye seemed hugely amused
by the whole thing.

"You ARE interesting Humans,"
he drawled. "I've never met Vikings
like this before. . . . You're tiny and not
very tough. You can't ski. You can't hunt. You can't
yell for toffee."

"Oh, shut up," snapped Hiccup crossly.

Fishlegs had fallen over exactly fifty-four times.
He was now covered with snow and wet through, and
his aim was not improved by a violent shivering. On
top of all this, he seemed to be catching a nasty cold.

A-A-C-H-O-O

"Oh this is HOPELESS!"
he exclaimed. "Absolutely
HOPELESS! A-A-ACHOOO!
Snotlout and Dogsbreath will have
probably murdered half the bird
population in the Archipelago by now and
we can't even get ourselves *one* measly Snowpecker
corpse! Why won't the wretched little birds stay still for
just a MILLISECOND?"

As Hiccup helped Fishlegs to his feet for the
fifty-fifth time, he thought he heard something almost
like deep human laughter. It seemed to be coming
from some distance below them, from behind a
snowdrift.

Leaving Fishlegs leaning on one of his poles,
warning Toothless to be quiet, Hiccup peered
cautiously over the top of the snowdrift.

And there, a hundred meters down the side of
yet another slope, was a sight that sent a nasty trickle
of fear down Hiccup's spine.

29

HYSTERICS.

Behind Hiccup's left shoulder, One Eye the Saber-Tooth growled grimly. The spines on his muscly back all stood up; his eyes narrowed. His tail with the spiky point swayed dangerously from side to side. "Now THOSE Humans," he hissed, "THOSE Humans really ARE Badder than most..."

"What's going on?" asked Fishlegs, wiping his runny nose on his sleeve, and rubbing his bottom, sore from falling over so often.

"Hysterics..." whispered Hiccup. "Get down..."

There were six Hysterics dressed in black sitting on the slopes below them. Five enormous stags lay dead on the ground beside them, their blood very red against the white snow. The Hysterics had clearly stopped for breakfast before the long ski back to the Hysterical Village on the other side of the Wrath of Thor. They had built a small fire, and were eating bits of deer in their fingers.

Their skis and their bows and arrows were jammed in the snow behind them.

"Thank Thor they haven't seen us," breathed Hiccup to Fishlegs. "Come on, we'll just ski quietly back the way we came."

This would have been an excellent plan.

But something weird was happening to Fishlegs.

He was already looking terrible, his eyes streaming and his nose running with snot. He was shaking a little with fever, and now as he watched the Hysterics, his face turned first pink, and then a brilliant red. He snorted furiously. "The Big Brainless Muscle-Bound Idiots!" he muttered.

"Yes, yes," whispered Hiccup, "but come on . . ."

"The murderers. . . . They've only gone and killed those poor deer in broad daylight . . . the great Stinking Gormless *Brutes* . . ."

"This is all true," said Hiccup, "but we need to get out of here before they kill *us* . . ."

But before Hiccup could stop him, Fishlegs had staggered to his feet and drawn his sword, crying out "COWARDS!!!!" at the top of his lungs.

The Hysterics stopped eating. They looked up in astonishment.

They couldn't have been more flabbergasted than Hiccup, as Fishlegs set off down the hill straight at the band of fearsome Warriors, in his lunatic uncontrolled slowplow. His ski poles flailed around frantically; his arrows flew out of their quiver like a hedgehog shedding needles; he was gaining speed every second, and shouting at the top of his voice:

"YOU MISERABLE MOLLUSKS! YOU WHIMPERING WINKLES! I COULD TAKE YOU FRITTERING FAIRY FOLK WITH ONE HAND BEHIND MY BACK! STAND AND FIGHT LIKE MEN, YOU COWARDLY COWERING CUTTLEFISH!"

FISHLEGS'S GUIDE ON HOW NOT TO SKI

Fig 1.
Wobble forward,
knees bent, bottom
out, determined
expression on face.

Fig 2. Whoops!
Slight ski crossorer
balance situation...

Fig 3.

Fall over.

Fig 4.

It is VERY IMPORTANT

to learn how to STOP.

3. THE HUNTERS BECOME THE HUNTED

Open-mouthed, almost in a trance, Hiccup watched the furious, frantic progress of his friend down the mountainside.

"YOU HORRIBLE HALITOSIS HADDOCK!" shrieked Fishlegs in a frenzy. "YOU PATHETIC PIECES OF PLANKTON! I CAN SEE YOU — YOU'RE BLUBBERING LIKE BABIES AT THE THOUGHT OF FIGHTING A REAL VIKING!"

One Eye, the Saber-Toothed Driver Dragon, was watching Fishlegs with something approaching awe. "You know, I underestimated your friend," he grunted respectfully. "I thought he was a complete weed, but I have to admit, that is BRAVE. . . . Suicidal, of course, but definitely brave . . ."

The Hysterics were so completely amazed to find themselves being attacked out of the blue by a single, undersized, underage member of another Tribe that for a moment they just froze, jaws hanging open, hands filled with deer halfway to their mouths.

Fishlegs skied straight at the Hysterics, swinging

his sword furiously when he got amongst them, but missing of course, and skiing straight over their campfire and on down the hill. For a moment his furs caught on fire, but the wind blew them out again.

The Hysterics paused for one second in their astonishment as they watched the small shrieking figure careening down the mountainside. They then looked at one another, and you didn't need to see their faces to know that it was a grim, Let's-Murder-Him-Now sort of look. They fastened on their skis in a businesslike, unhurried fashion, hoisted their bows on to their enormous hairy shoulders, and set off after him.

"Oh, by the Bouncing Buttocks of Beaming Baldur," panicked Hiccup, setting off down the slope after Fishlegs, "they're going to kill him, aren't they? What am I going to do?"

"Do?" asked One Eye, bounding beside Hiccup in long easy strides. "There's nothing you can do. . . . Your friend is as good as dead. . . . He's what we in the Saber-Tooth Pack would call a Walking Corpse . . . or a SKIING Corpse in his case. There's nothing you can do, and if you ski in this direction YOU may end up dead too . . ."

It looked like the dragon was right. Hiccup was

working hard to keep up with the Hysterics. Hysterics
are enormous and very strong skiers indeed.

And Fishlegs was traveling at a very fast speed
himself, on account of not doing anything fancy like
TURNING, admittedly totally out of control, and it
was amazing he hadn't fallen over already. Hiccup
could see him twisting his head every now and
again to shout more insults over his
shoulder.

The Hysterics were gaining, and one Big Brute
carrying a gigantic, double-headed, black and gold axe,
fastened an arrow to his bow.

Hiccup screeched to a stop, sending out a fan of
snow. He fixed an arrow to his own bow.

"Oh my horns and whiskers!" squealed
Toothless. "He's going to d-d-do something! Don't d-d-
do it, Hiccup! Don't do it!"

Hiccup took careful aim and let go of the arrow,
which sailed through the air, and hit the Big Brute with
the Axe, who was about to shoot Fishlegs, right bang
splat in the bottom.

It was the first successful hit
Hiccup had had all morning.

"Good shot!" roared
One Eye, enjoying
himself hugely.

The Big Brute with the
Axe let out a roar, and his arms flailed around wildly.
He let fly his own arrow, which, in a streak of glorious
luck, soared in a perfect arc . . . straight into the
bottom of the Hysteric skiing in front of him.

"Oh, this is too good . . . ," breathed One Eye.
"Pinch me. . . . It must be my birthday . . ."

That Hysteric then screamed in pain, and
pitched forward into a complete somersault, taking out
the Hysteric in front of *him*, who slid on his back into
the legs of the last three Hysterics, upturning them like
bowling pins, and all SIX Hysterics ended up in a
groaning, tangled, furious, snowy heap.

"Good, good," muttered Hiccup. "Now, please
make all six of them follow me, not Fishlegs."

"I think they will!" cried One Eye, crying with
laughter, "Oh, I think they will . . ."

"OVER HERE!" yelled Hiccup, making quite
sure they saw who had caused their downfall, and then

for good measure, "IF YOU'RE NOT AFRAID OF
BEING SHOT, YOU . . . WRIGGLING RUFFIAN
RUBBISH!"

"Look what you've d-d-done!" moaned Toothless.
"Those Hysterics are going to be so m-m-mad!"

Mad those Hysterics certainly were, as mad as
fire, and Hiccup set off down the mountain like a little
bolt of lightning.

"We've got a head start," panted Hiccup, skiing
faster than he ever had done in his entire life.

"But it's not going to be enough," gloated One
Eye with relish. "You've got half the mountain to ski
down, and they're going to catch up."

Sure enough, a horribly short time afterward,
Hiccup could hear the Hysterics beginning their
pursuit behind him.

Five of the Hysterics were howling the Hysterical
Howl like a pack of insane high-pitched wolves, and
the sixth, the one with the Axe, was screaming more
personal insults.

"How DARE you assault MY Royal Buttocks,
you midget Hooligan Assassin! We Hysterics are the
best Hunters in the entire world, and when I get hold
of you I shall chop you with my Chopper and feed you

41

to the Doomfang, I shall
shoot you full of arrows
and use you as a
colander!" yelled the
Hysteric with the Axe.

"Charming!" grinned One Eye.
"Fond of visitors, are they, the Hysterics?"

Hiccup headed straight for the woods,
thinking they would find it harder to shoot
him in there.

Now, skiing through a thickly
forested area is dangerous, hard

work, and the first rule you should follow in normal circumstances is to go SLOWLY.

These were not normal circumstances, and Hiccup screamed through that forest, madly twisting and turning, far too fast for safety.

"B-b-be careful!" warned Toothless helpfully. "M-m-mind the trees!"

"Oh thank you, Toothless," panted Hiccup sarcastically as he swerved violently this way and that, "I never thought of that . . ."

Dragons have quicker reflexes than humans, so One Eye and Toothless followed with ease. But the Hysterics weren't doing too badly either. Hiccup did hear one crash, as one of the Hysterics didn't turn in time and smashed into a tree.

But that left five Hysterics still chasing after him, and from the sound of their spine-creeping Hysterical Howls, getting closer by the second . . .

"You cannot get away!" screamed the Big Brute with the Axe. "When I get hold of you, I shall tear you limb from limb and use your wishbone as a toothpick!"

Meanwhile, down at the bottom of the gorge, Gobber had woken from his nap, and ten of his young pupils had returned from their hunting trip.

Gobber had harnessed five Saber-Toothed Drivers to the sleigh, and was waiting for the return of Hiccup and Fishlegs.

"I shot ninety Snowpeckers," boasted Speedifist to an impressed Wartihog.

"That's NOTHING," crowed Snotlout. "I got *two hundred and four* . . . easy-peasy lemon squeezy, it was like shooting fish in a barrel. Even Hiccup the Useless and his ridiculous Fishlegged friend must have got a few today; they can't be THAT pathetic."

"WHAT HAS HAPPENED TO THOSE NUMBSKULLS?" roared Gobber, beginning to feel a little uneasy. For Hiccup was the son of the Chief, Stoick the Vast, O Hear His Name and Tremble, Ugh, Ugh, and Stoick had a nasty temper and wouldn't be too pleased if anything had happened to his only son.

"Maybe they got ambushed by Snowpeckers?" sneered Snotlout.

There was a shouting from the gorge, and down it like an erratic snowplowing rocket came Fishlegs, arms whirring like windmills. Fishlegs was going so fast he couldn't possibly stop. He went on past the sleigh, past the openmouthed Gobber and the boys, and on and on for fifty meters until he eventually came to a stop, and collapsed on the ice.

Gobber ran after him, with a very nasty feeling now in the bottom of his stomach, and picked Fishlegs up.

Fishlegs looked terrible, purple and sweaty and trembling.

"HICCUP?" shouted Gobber. "WHERE is HICCUP?"

"Hysterics . . . ," gasped Fishlegs. "A . . . a . . . a . . . cchoo! *Hysterics* . . ."

Gobber turned as white as a Semi-Spotted Snowpecker.

Up above, Hiccup shot out of the cover of the trees like an arrow from a bow.

Directly below him was the gorge. . . . He could see the little speck of Gobber's sleigh, and little dots moving around it. The other boys must have made it back, then . . .

Hiccup knew that if he skied down the gorge, he would never make it. The Hysterics were so close behind him now they would shoot him or catch him before he reached the bottom.

He had to make a split-second decision.

Instead of heading toward the gorge, he set his teeth grimly and pointed his skis to the right, down the slope that led directly to the clifftop.

"What are you d-d-doing?" shrieked Toothless. "This w-w-way issa two-hundred-meter cliff! You going to d-d-die!"

Behind him, the Hysterics burst out of the woods. When they saw where Hiccup was going, they didn't even bother to start shooting. They just swooped after him, shouting out jeeringly:

"Where do you think *you're* going, Hooligan SCUM?"

"Say hello to Valhalla for me, because that's where you'll end up!"

They could see the edge of the cliff now, where the snow ended, and it was just an endless drop into nothingness.

"Stop!" shrieked Toothless. "S-s-stop!!"

"Why?" asked Hiccup. "I haven't got any choice. You think those Hysterics are going to give me a big warm hug and let me go?"

"N-n-no!" screamed Toothless. "But you can't ski off a c-c-cliff! Issa long way D-D-DOWN!"

"That's why I need your help, One Eye," said Hiccup to the great Saber-Toothed Dragon, who was bounding alongside.

"And what makes you think," sneered One Eye, "that I WANT to help you? I hate Humans. One less of you little pink slave drivers isn't going to trouble ME."

"That's true," said Hiccup, "but if I die, the next Chief of the Hairy Hooligan Tribe will be . . ."

Hiccup had run out of slope. He launched himself off the cliff, throwing his weight forward, skis wide apart. One Eye followed, unfolding his great wings.

"Will be who?" said One Eye urgently. "Will be who?" For one moment Hiccup soared up into that glorious infinity of blue sky like a bird.

49

And then he plunged DOWN.

"SNOTFACE"

yelled Hiccup as he fell.

Hiccup screamed
toward the ice at a hundred and
fifty miles per hour.

Gobber the Belch, watching from
below as the precious son of his Boss was about to
fall to his death, screamed as well.

In three seconds Hiccup would smash into the
ground and that would be the end of him.

After one second Hiccup was pretty sure One Eye
would save him. After two seconds he wasn't so sure.

And in fact the great Saber-Toothed Driver
Dragon was only just in time. For vital milliseconds his
hatred of humans held him back . . .

But then he folded back his wings and dived
after Hiccup.

A Saber-Tooth can dive more swiftly and beautifully than a peregrine falcon. One Eye caught Hiccup around the waist with his great talons in the nick of time, and then swept upward, wings stretched out like a great white kite. Hiccup gave a whoop of joy.

Down below, the watching boys cheered, and started the Hooligan Hurrah. Gobber practically *fainted*, such was his relief.

"Snotface Snotlout," said One Eye, as he spread his wings wide. "Is he the tall red-headed boy with a face like a pig?"

"That's the one," crowed Hiccup happily.

"Then you're right," replied One Eye, soaring even higher. "Perhaps you are one Human worth saving . . ."

Up on the clifftops, the Big Brute of a Hysteric with the Axe was so angry he snapped his ski poles like twigs. His furious voice floated up to them: "YOU'RE NOT SAFE YET! YOU'RE NOT SAFE EVER!" screamed the Big Brute, completely beside himself. "WHEREVER YOU GO I SHALL FIND YOU!

I SHALL FOLLOW YOU TO THE ENDS OF THE EARTH, TO THE BOTTOM OF THE OCEAN, IN THE GOD-LIKE HEIGHTS OF THE SKY! I PROMISE YOU, YOU HOOLIGAN COCKROACH, THAT YOU WILL REGRET THE DAY YOU SHOT AN ARROW IN THE BOTTOM OF NORBERT THE NUTJOB!" And then the sound became too faint for them to hear any more.

"Remind me," Hiccup said to Toothless as they flew along, "not to come back to Hysteria anytime in the next twenty years . . ."

"E-e-ever," replied Toothless passionately. "Not come back EVER."

Saber-Toothed Drivers are so bulky and muscular, they can only fly short distances, so One Eye dropped right down and placed Hiccup in the sleigh of a very relieved Gobber the Belch. Gobber took one look at the Hysterics on the clifftops, shaking their fists and howling the Hysterical Howl, and judged it might not be a good idea to stick around. He loaded Fishlegs and the other boys back onto the sleigh and, cheering and singing, they followed the flying Saber-Tooth all the way back to the little Isle of Berk.

I am the Venomous Vorpent,
Deadlier than an asp soaked in arsenic,
More toxic than toadstool-flavored tarantula.
Are you cough-y and cold-y and snotty and sneezy?
Are you mad? Are you sad? Do you feel queasy?
Is your skin so hot it is starting to smoke?
Is your throat so stiff it is making you choke?
If you fall down DEAD, perhaps you too
Have been stung by the VENOMOUS VORPENT.

Norbert
the **Nutjob**
finding Hiccup in his dreams.

4. IS THERE SOMETHING WRONG WITH FISHLEGS?

Hiccup did not sleep well that night. Every time he dropped off, Norbert the Nutjob found him in his dreams, screaming, "I will GRIND YOU INTO SAND! I WILL CHOP YOU WITH MY CHOPPER!" and Hiccup would wake up again, burningly hot and sweaty.

The following day, Toothless woke up in a furious temper because he still wasn't back in Hibernation Sleep. He'd done everything he should have done the night before. He'd gotten lots of exercise, drunk a milky drink at bedtime; all for nothing. On the dot of five o'clock the next morning, his greengage eyes opened up, SNAP, like a scallop opening its shell, and that was it for the day, no more sleeping.

And that was it for Hiccup too.

Toothless crawled up from his place at Hiccup's feet, like a small, enraged hot-water bottle. He stormed up Hiccup's body, digging his sharp little claws into Hiccup's tummy as he went, up to Hiccup's forehead, where he sat and hissed furiously.

"Toothless a-a-awake AGAIN. . . . 'Snot fair. . . .

IS it 5 o'clock ALREADY?

'Snot fair.... WHY
Toothless awake?
Everyone else a-a-
asleep ..."

It is not much
fun being woken up at
five o'clock in the morning
by a dragon sitting on your head and
hissing angry smoke rings straight up your nostrils.

"Well I'M awake now too," grumbled Hiccup,
coughing sleepily. "Could you blow those smoke rings
somewhere else; I've already got a sore throat ..."

"Oh you," fumed Toothless, blowing out great
clouds of furious smoke. "You're j-j-just a H-h-human,
you don't count.... Us d-d-dragons s-s-sensitive....
We n-n-need our sleep."

"Thank you, Toothless," said Hiccup through a
huge bout of coughing, "but we don't have to get up
now, you know, we can just doze for a bit ..."

Hiccup turned over onto his other side and
snuggled the furs more cozily around his shoulders, so
he could snooze for a bit longer.

But once Toothless was awake he was AWAKE.

56

The little dragon made a half-hearted pretense of snuggling down next to his Master, and then he bounced up again.

"Toothless get UP now . . . ," he said, flapping around Hiccup's head, tweaking his hair and blowing raspberries in his ears. "Issa l-l-lovely morning . . . come on . . . come on . . . Toothless h-h-hungry . . . Hiccup make Toothless b-b-breakfast . . ."

And when that didn't work, Toothless stood on Hiccup's shoulder, held his earlobe tenderly with one claw, and shrieked right down his ear hole, "MAYDAY MAYDAY! Toothless need to make p-p-pee-pee RIGHT NOW!"

Hiccup sat bolt upright like he'd been shot with an arrow. "Oh jumping jellyfish, not right now, Toothless, not on the bed again. . . . Hang on there, Toothless, just hang on . . ."

Hiccup jumped out of the bed in one hop, onto the freezing cold stone floor, and threw on four layers of furs, with Toothless flapping around his head squawking, "RIGHT NOW, RIGHT NOW, Toothless need pee-pee RIGHT NOW."

"Just hang on!" begged Hiccup. He had to take his mittens off to undo the big bolts on the front door,

Toothless shrieking, "Right now! Right now! Right now!"

Hiccup dragged open the door, and the day outside was still as dark as nighttime and very, very cold, so cold that the air was like an icy bucket of water being thrown in your face.

Toothless flew out, still shrieking, "Right now! Right now!" and squatted down on the snow a meter out of the front door.

"Well done for hanging on, Toothless," said Hiccup, banging his hands together to warm them up. Toothless squatted down, a look of pretend concentration furrowing his horns, but nothing seemed to be happening.

After a while Toothless got up. "Toothless NOT need p-p-pee-pee after all . . . ," he said decidedly.

Hiccup clapped his mittened hand to his forehead in frustration.

Sometimes being the owner of a dragon was VERY HARD WORK.

There was no point going back to bed now that he'd gotten up, so Hiccup fixed himself breakfast; and while he did this he had plenty of time to think.

Hiccup was worried about Fishlegs. Why had

Fishlegs attacked those Hysterics? It was very out of character. Normally Fishlegs would only have to get a *sniff* of something like a Hysteric and he would snowplow as quickly as possible in the opposite direction. OK, maybe all that falling over had set off his Berserk tendencies, but still, it was a bit peculiar . . .

And Fishlegs hadn't been looking too well, lately, either. Lots of sneezing and shivering, and *that* couldn't be caused by being a Berserk. It was almost like there was something WRONG WITH HIM . . .

An hour or so later, the door was flung open so wildly it nearly fell off its hinges, and Hiccup's father, Stoick the Vast, stomped into the room looking for his breakfast, like a six-and-a-half-foot earthquake, yawning so wide you could see his tonsils. Stoick the Vast was exactly what you might expect a Viking to be — loads of beard and not a lot of neck, masses of muscles but not a lot going on in the BRAIN department.

"Made some porridge, have you, son?" he roared. "Excellent, excellent." Stoick didn't bother putting the porridge into a bowl. He simply removed the cauldron from the fire, sat down at the table, and drank the porridge straight from the pot.

"Father?" said Hiccup.

"Mmm?" said Stoick absentmindedly, as he tipped his great head back and drank the last dregs of porridge, a lot of it running down his beard in a sticky, lumpy river.

"I wonder if you can help me. . . . I've been worrying about Fishlegs . . . ," said Hiccup.

Stoick finished the porridge with a great smacking of the lips and threw the cauldron into the fireplace with cheery violence.

"Is Fisheggs your odd little friend with the face like a depressed haddock?" boomed Stoick, grabbing a mackerel off the table and swallowing it, tail and head and eyes and all, in one gulp like a sword swallower swallowing swords.

"That's right," said Hiccup, "and his name isn't Fisheggs, it's Fish*legs* . . ."

"Well, there's a coinci-thingamajigy," bellowed Stoick.

"Do you mean coincidence?" asked Hiccup politely.

"Whatever" roared Stoick. "I'VE been worrying about Fisheggs too."

"You have?" asked Hiccup in surprise. It wasn't like Stoick to worry about *anything*.

"I have," said Stoick solemnly. "And I need to talk to you about something VERY SERIOUSLY. Come here, Hiccup."

Hiccup went and stood in front of his father. Chief Stoick put his hands on his son's shoulders and looked into his eyes very seriously. Hiccup tried to look serious too, but it is quite hard to take your father *totally* seriously when he seems to have a beard made entirely out of porridge.

"Son," said Stoick the Vast, "you are the son of a Chief, and the Heir to the Hooligan Tribe. A man is judged by the company he keeps, and I am sorry to have to tell you, but Fisheggs is the weirdiest little weirdo I have ever seen. You must give him up, Hiccup, give him up . . ."

"But, Father," protested Hiccup. "Fishlegs is my *friend*."

"SILENCE!" roared Stoick. And then more gently, "I know it is hard, son, but a Chief is a public figure. We Hooligans need to be FEARED by the other Tribes, so they don't start thinking they can

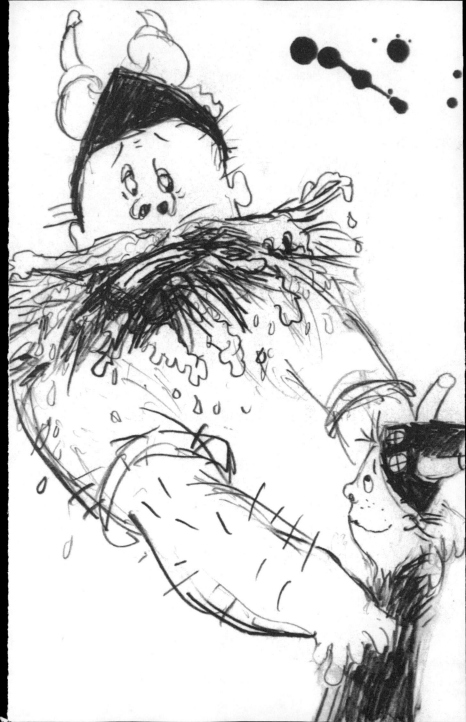

sneak along and invade us. . . . Fisheggs is a . . . well, let's face it, son, he's a bit ODD. You stand too near Fisheggs, son, and the Meatheads, and the Visithugs, and the Bog-Burglars and the Hysterics will start thinking YOU'RE a bit odd too . . . a bit soft, a bit WEAK, and then you're putting the whole Tribe in peril."

"Yes, Father," said Hiccup miserably.

"You need to start working on being TERRIFYING, Hiccup." Stoick patted his son on the shoulder, peering sympathetically at his sad face. This was hard, but it was for Hiccup's own good. "And Fisheggs isn't helping. Give him up, son. Your cousin, Snotlout, now, *there's* a suitable friend for you. Got an air of terrible danger about him. You stand shoulder to shoulder with Snotlout and you'll be feared throughout the Archipelago. Does that answer your question?"

"Yes, Father," said Hiccup very sadly.

Stoick the Vast clapped his son heartily on the back. "Good boy," roared Stoick. "I knew you'd see sense. And now, we'd better get ready for the Freya'sday Fete. . . . We don't want to be late now, do we? Old Wrinkly has given me a tip for the Young

Heroes Smashsticks-on-Ice Competition. . . . He's done some soothsaying,* and he tells me we Hooligans are going to win ten to two so I've put a bit of a bet on. Run and fetch your stick and skates, quick, boy."

Slowly, Hiccup went and fetched his Smashstick. Sadly, he picked up his ice skates.

"Old Wrinkly isn't very good at looking into the future," he warned his father, but Stoick wasn't listening.

Stoick rarely listened.

* Soothsaying means looking into the future

TOILET TRAINING

You: Toothless, ta COGLET me wantee ta cack-cack in di greenclaw crapspot...
Toothless, you KNOW I want you to poo in the dragon toilets...

Dragon: O yessee yessee, me coglet...
Yes, yes, I know...

You: (pointing at large poo in the middle of Stoick's bed) Erg... questa SA?
So what, then, is THIS?   PAUSE

Dragon (hopefully): Ummm... un chocklush snik-snak?
Er... a chocolate biscuit?

You: Snotta chocklush snik-snak, issa CACK-CACK, issa cack-cack di Toothless NA in di greenclaw crapspot, may oopla bang splosh in di middling di sleepy-slab di pappa.
This isn't a chocolate biscuit, it's a POO, it's one of YOUR poos, Toothless, and it ISN'T in the dragon toilets, it's right bang splat in the middle of my father's bed.

CELEBRATE THE COMING OF SPRING AT THE

FREYA'SDAY FETE

PROGRAM OF EVENTS

10:00 Young Heroes Smashsticks-On-Ice competition on the frozen harbor. No rules. No quarter given. No survivors. No limits.

11:00 Mud Wrestling. Can Big-Boobied Bertha be the All-In-Snow-Wrestling Champion for the third year in a row? Will those boobies remain undefeated?

12:00 Have a go at the FROZEN LUCKY DIP. We have frozen 500 everyday objects into 500 identical lumps of ice. Can you guess what they are and take something useful home?

5. SMASHSTICKS-ON-ICE

The Freya'sday Fete took place every year on
Freya'sday Eve, which was the Viking holiday
celebrating the end of winter and the coming of spring.

This year the Fete was being held out in the
middle of the frozen sea in Hooligan Harbor. It was
strange to think that only six months before the
Harbor had been filled with a grey, surly ocean. Now
there were red and white striped tents pitched
higgledy-piggledy all over the ice. Roaring fires burned
high, grilling Semi-Spotted Snowpeckers for the
Vikings to munch on as they wandered around stalls
selling octopus lollipops, or listened to storytellers
telling tall stories, or watched openmouthed as the
giants on skates balanced dwarves on their heads.

There was a big area marked
out for the Smashsticks-on-Ice
Competitions. Smashsticks-on-Ice
was a very rough and complicated
game played with bats, balls, and
ice skates. Nobody was quite
sure of the rules, which meant

that people tended to make them up as they went along, and then anybody who complained would start a fight.

The Young Heroes were supposed to go first, followed later on by the Adult Warriors. They would be playing against another Tribe, the Bog-Burglars, who had been invited over to join in the Celebrations for the day.

The Bog-Burglars were a Tribe of fearsome female Warriors who lived on an island some way to the west. Their Chief, Big-Boobied Bertha, stood nearby, gulping down mugs of beer and scratching her chin stubble.

Her daughter, Camicazi, a very small girl with a swagger and the tangliest hair in the Inner Isles, was practicing swinging her Smashstick.

Camicazi was a friend of Hiccup's, and he wandered over to ask her if she had seen Fishlegs that morning.

"Nope," said Camicazi cheerily. "But I hope you Hooligan boys are feeling lucky. We Bog-Burglars are going to MURDER you weedy little BOYS in the Smashsticks. I bet you Hooligans are hopeless at it —

69

apart from you, of course, Hiccup," she added.
Camicazi had a great admiration for Hiccup, ever since
he had rescued her from being eaten by Sharkworms
in Fort Sinister. *

Snotlout happened to be skating past at that

*This takes place in "How to Speak
Dragonese," another of Hiccup's memoirs

Big-Boobied Bertha
in holiday mood...

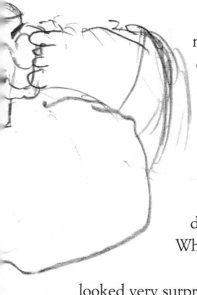

moment and he nearly fell over, he laughed so much at this. "Hiccup???" jeered Snotlout. "*Hiccup* will get as many goals as he shot Semi-Spotted Snowpeckers yesterday. *I* shot more than two hundred. How many did you shoot, again, Hiccup? What was it — none??"

Hiccup blushed. Camicazi looked very surprised.

"P-P-ARP! The Young Heroes Smashsticks-on-Ice Match is about to begin! Please could both teams make their way to the ice . . . ," shouted Gobber the Belch from the center of the ice.

Gobber had changed into his shortest shorts to be the referee. The Bog-Burglars (apart from Camicazi,

of course) were big, rough, mean-looking girls with
wild hair, broken noses, and thighs like tree trunks.

Fishlegs staggered onto the ice at the last
minute. He looked even more terrible than the last

time Hiccup saw him. He was sneezing and shivering hard, and he could hardly stand, and was using his Smashstick to hold himself up. He had put his ice skates on the wrong feet.

Hiccup put up his hand to try and get Gobber's attention. "Sir, I think Fishlegs isn't well," he said.

"NONSENSE!" roared Gobber. "Vikings don't get SICK! Flu is for softies! Colds are for babies! Plagues are for girlies! I'VE never had a day's sickness in all my life, not even a sore throat. I don't want to hear ANOTHER WORD."

Hiccup and Fishlegs skated out onto the ice, Hiccup supporting Fishlegs, who could hardly put one skate in front of the other.

"You ought to be at home," worried Hiccup. "You look awful."

Fishlegs laughed sarcastically. "Didn't you hear Gobber? Vikings don't get SICK. . . . I'm not ill, I'm just shivering with EXCITEMENT to be out here on this frostbitingly cold day . . ."

Gobber blew the whistle, threw the puck into the Smashstick Scrum, and all hell broke loose.

Ten boys and girls fell on top of one
another in an untidy hairy mess, clonking each
other on the head with their wooden sticks. Within two
minutes Wartihog, Clueless, Lovethug, and Deadly
Doris were lying stretched out on the ice, and
Camicazi had somehow broken free of the scrum and

was skating toward Hiccup and Fishlegs
at breakneck speed. Fishlegs moved in
to tackle her, and she pulled his helmet over
his eyes so he couldn't see anything, before
skillfully shooting the puck between the goalposts.

And as the Bog-Burglars merrily cried out,

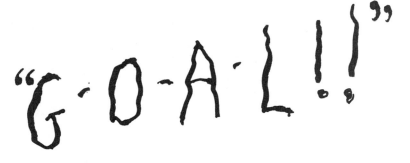

"G·O-A·L!!"

an extraordinary change came over Fishlegs.

He tore off his helmet and he snorted like a bull
about to charge.

"Uh-oh," said Hiccup. He had seen that look
somewhere before. "Now hang on a second, Fishlegs,
don't do anything rash . . ."

"FOUL!" bellowed Fishlegs.

Fishlegs skated toward the gigantic figure of the
referee, Gobber the Belch, like a crab slipping on soap.

"GOBBER, YOU BIG, STUPID, BARBARIAN BABOON, ARE YOU **BLIND**? SHE FOULED ME!"

Gobber started, as surprised as if a small pink prawn on a plate had suddenly leapt up and bit him.

"**WHAT** did you say, Fishlegs????" roared Gobber in astonishment.

"SOMETHING WRONG WITH YOUR EARS AS WELL AS YOUR EYES?" screamed Fishlegs. "I'VE MET **SHEEP** MORE INTELLIGENT THAN YOU ARE! I'VE MET **JELLYFISH** WHO COULD OUTPLAY YOU IN A GAME OF CHESS!"

Gobber swelled up like a balloon about to explode.

"**I'LL DEAL WITH THIS, BELCH!**" yelled Stoick the Vast, skating ponderously over to this extraordinary scene.

Stoick the Vast looked down at Fishlegs from the giant height of six and half feet.

"YOUNG MAN," he roared,

"YOUR CHIEFTAIN IS
SPEAKING TO YOU. THIS IS A
SPECIAL OCCASION. . . .
THERE ARE BOG-BURGLARS
PRESENT." Stoick pointed to the Bog-
Burglars, who were killing themselves
laughing.

Fishlegs was silent for a second, looking
up at his Chieftain. And then . . .

"FATTY!" shrieked Fishlegs.

Stoick the Vast started.

"LARDY-BUM!" shouted Fishlegs. "WHO'S
BEEN HAVING TOO MANY SECOND
HELPINGS, CHIEF GREEDIGUTS OF THE
JELLY-BELLIES??"

Stoick the Vast turned as red as a lobster.
"HOW **DARE** YOU TALK TO YOUR CHIEF IN
THIS RUDE AND IMPERTINENT MANNER?"

Fishlegs opened his mouth to scream some more
insults, but Hiccup interrupted.

"He's not well, Father," whispered Hiccup
urgently. "I think his Berserk thingy has gone wrong. . . .
Please, Father . . . I'll take him home, he's not well . . ."

"Take him home, then," growled Stoick to Hiccup. "But I'm warning you, son, that boy isn't fit to be a Hooligan, let alone a friend to the son of the Chief."

At first Fishlegs didn't want to be dragged away, but while he was struggling, he fell over, and the cold shock of landing in the snow brought him back to his senses again.

Hiccup was really worried now, and he decided to take Fishlegs to Old Wrinkly, to see whether HE knew what was wrong . . .

Old Wrinkly's Cures for Common Illnesses

ILLNESS	
COLD	Stuff a small carrot up each nostril to stop a running nose. Remember to breathe through MOUTH.
UPSET STOMACH	Drink a cupful of live earwigs. The insects will attack the germs in your small intestine and eat them. Probably.
CHICKEN POX	Paint the spots with Old Wrinkly's soothing lotion of Runny Seagull Poo. This will relieve the itching. It will also cause your friends to stay away from you, thus protecting them from infection.
HEADACHE WITH TEMPERATURE	Old Wrinkly's tasty medicine of sheep mucus and dead flies wrapped in cobwebs will soon have the patient bouncing out of bed.
A VIRUS	Pray to Thor. Nobody knows what to do with a virus. *

* Interestingly, 1,500 years later, medical science has advanced to such an extent, that we STILL don't know what to do with a virus.

6. WHAT OLD WRINKLY SAID

Old Wrinkly was Hiccup's grandfather on his mother's side. He lived in a large untidy house on the beach. He was delighted to see them, and he fed them all porridge. Toothless snoozed in front of the blazing fire in his fireplace, while the snowy clothes of Hiccup and Fishlegs dripped dry on chairs.

"What can I do for you, little Hiccup?" wheezed Old Wrinkly, lighting a big fat pipe.

"It's my friend, Fishlegs," explained Hiccup. "He's not very well."

Old Wrinkly looked at Fishlegs, who was shaking like a leaf in a high wind.

"Oh come on, Hiccup," said Fishlegs irritably. "I keep telling you, it's just a NASTY COLD . . ."

Old Wrinkly tut-tutted.

Old Wrinkly was the wise man and soothsayer of the Hooligan Tribe. If you were ill, you would go to Old Wrinkly and he would examine you, consult the gods, and then give you some perfectly disgusting medicine like rabbits' droppings in limpet goo that might or might not make you better. (Doctoring and looking into the future are complicated businesses — to tell the truth, Old Wrinkly did not always get them right.)

Old Wrinkly put his ancient old hand on Fishlegs's forehead, and tut-tutted again. "Very hot, very hot," he muttered to himself, "and sweaty." He listened to Fishlegs's heart with a strange trumpetlike instrument and tut-tutted some more.

And then he threw some twigs onto the fire, and poked the flames with a long metal stick.

"Oh dearie me!" gasped Old Wrinkly as he stared at the red embers.

"That sounds cheerful," shivered Fishlegs.

"The fire seems to be telling me that your friend has VORPENTITIS, caused by the sting of a VENOMOUS VORPENT," said Old Wrinkly sadly. "Have you met any Venomous Vorpents recently?"

There was a nasty cold feeling in the bottom of Hiccup's stomach.

"We *did* meet a Venomous Vorpent . . . ," Hiccup said slowly. "A couple of months ago . . . a Vorpent fell onto Fishlegs's hand when we were escaping from Fort Sinister . . ."

"But it didn't sting me!" Fishlegs said eagerly. "I didn't feel anything sting me!"

Old Wrinkly shook his head. "The Vorpent numbs the skin before it stings. It's very clever really. You wouldn't have felt a thing. And then nothing happens, until a couple of months later, when you fall ill with Vorpentitis."

"What are the symptoms of Vorpentitis?" asked Hiccup.

"Fever . . . runny nose . . . episodes of madness . . ." replied Old Wrinkly gloomily.

Hiccup's stomach was now as cold as ice, but he tried to sound cheerful. "And how do we get him better?"

Old Wrinkly sounded gloomier still. "Weeeell . . . ," he croaked, "that's the tricky part. . . . The sting of the Venomous Vorpent is pretty much always FATAL."

There was a nasty silence.

"The good news is," continued Old Wrinkly, "we have until ten in the morning tomorrow to find the antidote* before your friend dies."

"Oh good," said Hiccup, hugely relieved. "So there IS an antidote . . ."

 * an antidote is a CURE

Fishlegs had been listening with an open mouth. "But all I've got is a NASTY COLD!" he protested. "A nasty cold — and you tell me I've only got one day to live!"

Hiccup ignored him. "What's the antidote?" asked Hiccup.

"This is where the tricky part gets trickier . . ." wheezed Old Wrinkly. "The antidote to the sting of the Venomous Vorpent is *the Vegetable-That-No-One-Dares-Name.*"

"What, you mean the POTATO?" gasped Hiccup.

"Sssssh," whispered Old Wrinkly, desperately flapping his hands. *"You're not supposed to name it! It's bad luck!"*

"But the POTATO is an *imaginary* vegetable!" said Hiccup, who thought all this talk of bad luck was just superstition. "It doesn't really exist!" *

"There *are* those that say the Vegetable-That-No-One-Dares-Name can be found in a great country to the west known as America . . . ," Old Wrinkly pointed out.

"But most people say," said Hiccup slowly, "that

* Potatoes only grew in America at this time, and America hadn't been discovered yet.

there's no such place as America. Most people say that it's an imaginary land that only crackpot weirdos believe in. Most people think that the earth is as flat as a pancake, and if you sail too far to the west you will fall off the end of it."

"That *is* what most people say," admitted Old Wrinkly, shrugging his shoulders and carrying on puffing his pipe.

"And even if there WAS such a thing as this so-called potato in this so-called land called America," argued Hiccup, "we're never going to be able to sail to it and find the antidote in only ONE DAY. In one day you'd hardly be out of the Sullen Sea. . . . The thing you're suggesting is IMPOSSIBLE."

"There's no such thing as im-POSSIBLE, Hiccup," snorted Old Wrinkly, "only im-PROBABLE. The only thing that limits us are the limits to our imaginations . . . and *I* used to think of you as an imaginative boy. Give up, if you want to . . . but *I* used to think of you as the sort of boy who would NEVER give up, however bad things looked."

"OK, then," said Hiccup crossly. "Give me *one* reason not to give up."

"I will give you a reason," said Old Wrinkly. "There is a chance that Norbert the Nutjob, Chief of the Hysterics, may have the antidote to Vorpentitis."

Hiccup jumped. "NORBERT THE NUTJOB??" said Hiccup. "Why does HE have a POTATO? Where did he get it from?"

"I will explain by telling you the story of Norbert the Nutjob's father and the Doomfang," said Old Wrinkly.

"You do that," said Hiccup, already feeling anxious at the mere *mention* of Norbert the Nutjob.

Old Wrinkly relit his pipe. "I have to warn you, Hiccup," wheezed Old Wrinkly between puffs, "that, like a lot of stories, this may or *may not* be true . . ."

The Story of Norbert the Nutjob's Father and the Doomfang

"Fifteen years ago," began Old Wrinkly, *"the Chief of the Hysterical Tribe was Norbert the Nutjob's father, Bigjob. . . . The Hysterics have never believed that the world is flat, and that if you sail too far to the west you will fall off the end of it. The Hysterics think this is poppycock. Bigjob believed that the earth was as round as the moon, and he set out to prove it.*

"Bigjob built the greatest Viking ship you have ever seen, a ship called The American Dream, *and he sailed far, far to the west through storms as black and wild as Woden's nightmares. He sailed past icebergs higher than a ship's great mast and on and on over the Great Green Sea Desert, and however far he sailed he never came to the end of the world, for the world is as round as a circle, and a circle has no end."*

87

Hiccup could contain himself no longer. "Is this true?" he burst out. "Is the world *really* a circle that has no end?"

"I have no idea," replied Old Wrinkly calmly. "As I told you, this is a story. Be quiet and I'll tell you the end.

"After a journey so long it seemed like forever, Bigjob at last found the land that he had dreamed about, the land called America. This was a glorious country, full of natural Treasures like the Vegetable-That-No-One-Dares-Name, and friendly natives that Bigjob called 'Feather People.' Bigjob spent a happy couple of months there before returning home to the Inner Isles.

"Norbert's father decided to take back with him a FROZEN VEGETABLE-THAT-NO-ONE-DARES-NAME, so that everybody would believe that he really had been to America. On the journey back, Bigjob had an extraordinary feeling the ship was being FOLLOWED. At first he thought it was a great whale or a shark, but eventually he realized it was something far, far worse. It was a tremendous Sea Dragon called a DOOMFANG."

"That *is* strange," interrupted Hiccup. Hiccup knew a great deal about dragons, and this was very odd behavior for a Doomfang. Doomfangs are heavily armed, terrifying creatures, but they normally just ignore humans.

"Will you stop interrupting?" said Old Wrinkly.

"This dreadful animal followed them all the way from America like a Curse. It was only when they reached the Wrath of Thor that the animal attacked, and tried to swallow the boat. Bigjob was very brave. Riding his dragon the Thunderer, he shot arrow after arrow at the Doomfang. These specially sharp arrows had been given to Bigjob by the Feather People, who are very expert at making arrows. Bigjob was down to his last arrow when the Doomfang finally killed him. Ever since that day, the Doomfang has never left the

*Wrath of Thor. For fifteen years, no one has been
able to get into Hysteria, and no one can come out.
The Chief of the Hysterical Tribe is now Bigjob's
son, Norbert the Nutjob, and he has never
gotten over the death of his father. It is said
that he keeps the frozen Vegetable-That-No-
One-Dares-Name in a casket, and it is in as
good condition as it was fifteen years ago.*

"So there you are," said Old Wrinkly,
"That is the story of Norbert the Nutjob's father
and the Doomfang. Of course, at this time of year, the
Wrath of Thor is frozen over, and the Doomfang is
trapped under the ice. And Hysteria is only a three-
hour sleigh ride from here."

Hiccup jumped to his feet. "I know," he said. "We
were there only yesterday. We haven't got a moment to
lose. . . . I must go to Hysteria and bring back the
antidote."

Fishlegs's mouth dropped open. "I can't believe
I'm hearing this. . . . You're thinking of GOING BACK
TO HYSTERIA??? The creepiest, grimmest, scariest
place I have ever been to in all my life, and you're going
to go there in the DARK?"

"The Hysterics won't see me coming in the dark," Hiccup pointed out.

"You shot Norbert the Nutjob in the bottom with an ARROW!" howled Fishlegs. "You think you can just ask him politely to give you his precious American vegetable and he's just going to HAND IT OVER??"

"Burglary may be involved," admitted Hiccup.

"And all because of Old Wrinkly's SOOTH-SAYING? Everybody knows that Old Wrinkly is nearly as hopeless at soothsaying as you are at Frightening Foreigners."

"Thank you," murmured Old Wrinkly.

Fishlegs hadn't finished yet. "I keep on telling you . . . I have just got a BAD COLD. . . . A . . . a . . . a . . . tish-yoo! Actually, I'm not feeling that well. . . . Would you mind if I lie down for a moment?"

"Be my guest," said Old Wrinkly. "You can have *my* bed . . . and I'll make you some hot lemon and honey. Don't forget, Hiccup, you have until ten in the morning tomorrow, before Fishlegs dies . . . TEN in the morning, mind . . ."

So Hiccup left Old Wrinkly looking after his great

friend Fishlegs, and ran out of the door. He had finally realized he might not have much time left . . .

And although he didn't know it at the time, those were the first steps he took toward the scariest, the most alarming and ghastly adventure of his life so far. He was indeed setting out on a quest . . . a quest that would be a race against time and lead him to a terrifying monster and icy peril, which would be sung about by bards ever after as the *Quest for the Frozen Potato*.

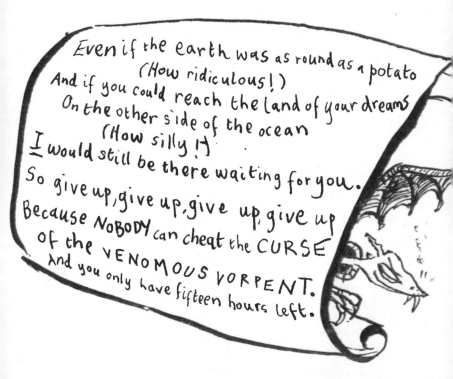

Even if the earth was as round as a potato
(How ridiculous!)
And if you could reach the land of your dreams
On the other side of the ocean
(How silly!)
I would still be there waiting for you.
So give up, give up, give up, give up
Because NOBODY can cheat the CURSE
of the VENOMOUS VORPENT.
And you only have fifteen hours left.

7. THE QUEST FOR THE FROZEN POTATO

Hiccup marched out of Old Wrinkly's house back to the Celebrations in the Harbor, followed by a grumbling Toothless. For about six hundred meters he was absolutely certain about what he was going to do.

He would go and explain to his father what had happened, and ask him to set up a Quest for the Frozen Potato. The Hooligans were always going on quests.

But when he eventually found his father, who was trying his luck in the Frozen Lucky Dip, he suddenly didn't feel quite so sure of himself.

Stoick wasn't as pleased to see his only son as he normally was. He had just lost a big bet because the Bog-Burglar Young Heroes had **WHIPPED** the Hooligan Young Heroes in the Smashsticks on-Ice Competition, fourteen goals to nil. So Stoick was not in the best of moods.

"*Bother* that Old Wrinkly and his stupid soothsaying. An **EASY WIN** for the Hooligans, he said. Put all your money on it, he said. And what happens? The Bog-Burglars win fourteen–NIL. I should have known it," Stoick muttered to himself as he drew a large frozen object from the lucky dip and tried to work out what it was. Fish? A useful axe? A small chair?

"Father," said Hiccup determinedly, "I want to set out on a quest."

Stoick looked at his son with surprise. "What sort of quest?"

"You remember my friend Fishlegs?" said Hiccup.

Stoick rubbed his nose crossly and grunted.

"Old Wrinkly says the reason he attacked you was because he has been stung by the Venomous Vorpent and he is in the first stage of Vorpentitis, and that causes episodes of madness, you know . . . and the thing is, Father, unless we can find the antidote in time Old Wrinkly says Fishlegs may DIE . . ."

Stoick looked as if he wasn't sure whether to be sad or happy . . . but then he saw his son's face and hurriedly looked sad.

"Um . . . yes . . . oh *dear* . . . ," said Stoick.

"So I want to set out on a quest for the antidote," announced Hiccup.

"What is the antidote?" asked Stoick the Vast.

"Old Wrinkly says the antidote is the potato," said Hiccup.

"SSSSSShhhh!" said Stoick. "You're not supposed to name it! And the Vegetable-That-No-One-Dares-Name is an *imaginary* vegetable — surely you know that, Hiccup?"

"Old Wrinkly says that the Hysterics went to America and brought back a frozen potato," continued Hiccup stubbornly. "So I want to FIND the potato and save Fishlegs's life."

"I FORBID YOU TO DO ANY SUCH THING!" roared Stoick.

"If we don't believe in the potato Fishlegs may DIE!" Hiccup yelled right back at his father.

Stoick the Vast lost his temper and waved the Unidentified Frozen Object (U.F.O.) around his head.

He roared at his son so loudly poor Hiccup's ears rang.

"YOUR FRIEND FISHLEGS IS A LITTLE WEIRDO WHO JUST CALLED ME A JELLY-BELLIED LARDY-BOTTOMED GREEDIGUTS!"

Hiccup flinched as if he had been struck, and then Stoick felt ashamed, and controlled himself. He reached out and patted his son on the shoulder, and he tried to speak more reasonably.

"Look, son, I know this is difficult for you, because you are fond of your friend, but let's just say that for once in a blue moon Old Wrinkly is right. Even then, as the Chief I WILL NOT risk the life of my only son for the sake of a little weirdo that Fate has got it in for."

"Isn't it the Chief's *job* to do that?" said Hiccup steadily. "Fishlegs has no one else to look after him."

"You WILL NOT do it," said Stoick, very meaningfully indeed. "Because I FORBID it, and that is an order, son. An order from your CHIEF." Stoick put the U.F.O. on his head (he had decided it was a HELMET) and stalked off.

The unfortunate thing about going on a quest to save the life of your sick best friend is that you have no best friend to go *with* you. Hiccup watched his father stalking off with what looked very like a frozen chair on his head, and wondered miserably what his chances were if he went on the quest for the Frozen Potato alone.

Not im-POSSIBLE, he thought sadly, but, let's face it, im-PROBABLE.

Camicazi stuck her head out from underneath the Lucky Dip table.

"Did I hear someone mention the word quest? When do we get started?"

"Oh, Camicazi. . . . You really shouldn't listen in on other people's conversations," said Hiccup.

Camicazi wriggled out from underneath the table and started doing handstands. She still had her ice skates on.

"We Bog-Burglars always listen in on other people's conversations," she said cheerfully. "It's one of the reasons I'm going to be so helpful to you on the quest for the Frozen Potato."

"YOU are not going on the quest for the Frozen Potato," said Hiccup. "It's far too dangerous."

"Dangerous? PAH!" boasted Camicazi. "Why, I've burgled whole flocks of SHEEP off the Visithugs. . . . I've picked the pockets of the Perilous

Pirates. . . . I've stolen the helmet right off the head of Madguts the Murderous, and you want me to steal *one measly little vegetable*?? No problemo, Hiccup, watch and learn, my boy, watch and learn."

Hiccup raised his eyes to the heavens. If Camicazi had a fault, it was that she was very, very pleased with herself. But it had to be admitted, she was an excellent burglar.

"There's this Madman with an Axe . . . ," Hiccup pointed out.

"Better and better," said Camicazi. "There's nothing I enjoy *more* than teasing Madmen with Axes. It's my favorite sport. If you don't let me join in I'll tell your big fat cross father where you're going."

"But that's blackmail!" protested Hiccup.

"You see," grinned Camicazi, "we Bog-Burglars have no morals at all. It's very useful to us."

Hiccup gave up, and said she could come if she wanted to.

Camicazi rushed off to get her burglary equipment, and Hiccup prepared a small sleigh to take them to Hysteria.

He also pulled down his boat, *The Hopeful Puffin*, to drag on runners behind the sleigh.

"What *are* you doing?" asked Camicazi, returning with her arms laden with ropes and oddly shaped, pointy metal objects.

"It's getting so near to springtime, the ice may start cracking when we're out there. And if it does we're going to need some way of getting back across the Sullen Sea," replied Hiccup, trying not to think about what would happen if the ice REALLY DID melt. That might mean they had to face the Doomfang, on top of all their other problems.

Hiccup went off to look for One Eye, and explained his problem, and the big Driver laughed sneerily.

"Look, revolting little Human boy, I don't know why you think I might want to help you. I am not your mommy. I HATE humans. One thing I will absolutely SWEAR to you. I will NEVER, repeat NEVER, waste a tear crying over the death of one of you Human No-Brainers."

"Ah," said Hiccup cunningly, "but the antidote isn't just going to save the life

ropes for climbing and swinging on

knapsack for burgled items

lots of secret pockets

sword

...hings for ...icking ...ocks

tiny dagger for emergencies

protective goggles

spiked shoes for extra GRIP

Camicazi's Burglary Equipment

of my friend Fishlegs, is it?
The Vorpent stings dragons as
well as humans. Thousands of DRAGONS
die of Vorpentitis every year. When I
bring back the frozen potato, I shall plant
potatoes all over Berk, and no dragon
shall die of Vorpentitis ever again."

Well, that got One Eye, of course,
because his hatred of humans was
only matched by his love for his fellow dragons,
and five minutes later Hiccup was hitching
the big Saber-Toothed Dragon
up to his sleigh.

Hiccup told Stoick on the way that
he was going to spend the night at Snotlout's
house, and Stoick was delighted.

"Excellent, my boy," roared Stoick, "so you've
decided to take my advice, and find yourself a better
friend. Well done, Hiccup."

"So now," said Hiccup, sitting down
in the sleigh next to Camicazi, "we can nip to Hysteria,
steal the potato, and get it to Fishlegs without my
father even knowing we've gone."

Only Snotlout noticed the small Sleigh-Dragging-a-Boat sneaking out of Hooligan Harbor, on its way to Hysteria on the quest for the Frozen Potato.

Snotlout hoped that wherever Hiccup was going, it was somewhere dangerous, and that he would NEVER COME BACK.

8. THE WRATH OF THOR

One Eye pulled the sleigh across the ice at a crazy
speed. Once or twice Hiccup tugged on the reins to try
and get him to slow down, but the big Driver ignored
him, and so in the end, Hiccup gave up trying. "The
quicker we get to Hysteria, the better, anyway," he
reminded himself. The burningly cold wind slammed
into his face, tearing at his eyelids as they careened
across the ice.

The Hopeful Puffin bounced crazily behind
them like an ugly duckling desperately trying to keep
up with its demented mother. Luckily, although she
was not an attractive-looking boat, she was sturdy and
used to the odd knock or two. Hiccup had brought
along snacks for everybody that were supposed to last
the whole journey, but Toothless finished all of them in

the first three minutes, littering the sleigh with crumbs, chicken bones, and nut shells.

"Toothless c-c-cold . . . ," he wailed. "Toothless h-h-hungry. . . . Toothless BORED. Ow ow ow ow . . . Camicazi s-s-sitting on my ta-a-ail. . . . Are we nearly there yet?"

"We only left five minutes ago!" exclaimed Hiccup.

"Toothless play I-Spy," said Toothless firmly.

At first Camicazi was horribly cheerful, chatting constantly, and singing loudly, her bright blue eyes prickling with excitement.

But as the long hours wore on, and as they played their fifty-second game of I-Spy with Hiccup translating for Toothless, and as the sky turned pink and grey with the coming of the evening, and as they passed the Mazy Multitudes to their left and began to hear the first moans of the Doomfang under the ice, even Camicazi fell silent.

Hiccup made One Eye wait for the evening to grow darker before they turned the corner into the Wrath of Thor, so the Hysteric lookouts wouldn't spot them coming.

For a tense,
stomach-churning half hour they
waited, until Hiccup judged it was
safe, and gave a pull on One Eye's
reins to get him going again.

The gigantic sea cliffs of Villainy
and Hysteria loomed above them
scarily in the darkness. One Eye bounded into the
Wrath of Thor, and the cliffs leapt up on either side
of the little sleigh as it raced along, like dizzyingly high
prison walls.

The eyes of dragons shine in the dark, and so
One Eye's great eye acted as a searchlight,
showing them the way. The ice in the narrow
gorge was so clear that it was almost
transparent, and in the beam of One Eye's eye,
you could see right through it, as if it were a
two-meter-thick pane of frosted glass, down
into the sea below. How
interesting, thought Hiccup
as he looked over the edge
of the sleigh; I can even

make out a
shoal of mackerel
down there . . .

The mass of tiny fish went on forever,
swimming slowly in their millions way
down below them, until suddenly they
fled, shooting away like tiny sparks in an
explosion, as a great dark shape, infinitely
large, suddenly appeared under the ice. It was the
gargantuan shadow of a dragon the size of an
underwater mountain, and it easily kept up with
the speedy little sleigh, its long tail lazily
powering it along, its wings nearly
brushing the edges of the Wrath of
Thor as it beat them slowly to swim
underneath.

"Issa D-d-doomfang!"
whispered Toothless into Hiccup's
ear. "Let's go h-h-home . . ."

Hiccup gazed downward in
fascinated horror as the great dragon
turned its head to one side and Hiccup

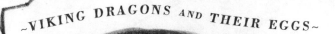

The DOOMFANG

The Doomfang is a gigantic predator of the Open Ocean, very rarely seen by humans. It is armed not only with fearsome fangs and claws, but also a strange blue fire that "freezes" its victims to death.

~STATISTICS~

COLORS: Always as black as your darkest nightmare.

ARMED WITH: Terrible jaws and fangs. Also have unusual frozen fire breath, with blue flames that kill by FREEZING you... 30

RADAR: Yes...... 10

POISON: None...... 0

HUNTING ABILITY: Unbeatable skills...... 30

SPEED: Very, very fast...... 25

FEAR AND FIGHT FACTOR: Terrifying....30

found himself staring into an enormous, bloodshot, green dragon eye, as long as the sleigh itself.

It was as if all the green in the world, of peas, of grass, of spinach, of leaves, of beans and frogs, had been concentrated in that one eye and given it the intensity of a pure green acid. It was like looking straight into the sun at midday, through a great green microscope, and Hiccup was so dazzled he nearly fell off the sleigh, until he was brought back to his senses by a terrible **THUD!** and the ice below them jumped up like an earthquake. The sleigh jumped too, and One Eye soared briefly into the air with a complaining yowl.

THUD! went the ice again as the Doomfang butted his head against the thick transparent wall. With terrified relief, Hiccup realized the ice was so deep that it was holding strong, although it was now shot through with tiny little white cracks.

The sleigh raced toward the entrance to Hysteria Harbor like a mouse streaking toward a mousehole. The dragon followed, the ice thudding underneath as they went, with terrible blows from its battering-ram head. When One Eye turned into the harbor, he was going so fast the momentum from the boat behind almost turned them around in a great screeching circle. The sleigh balanced wildly on one runner, before slamming back down and carrying on.

Hiccup looked over his shoulder. The Doomfang was too large to fit through the narrow harbor entrance. It pushed its great head through and Hiccup could see, though not hear, its huge mouth opening in a roar of rage, its paw with the terrible talons tearing at the water. It blew out a great gush of underwater blue flame that shot out underneath the speeding sleigh and streaked forward in a straight line right up to the shoreline, almost as if it were a bright blue road telling them where to go.

"He's not pleased," joked Camicazi as the sleigh raced along the bright blue road. "That is one Doomfang in a VERY BAD MOOD."

"Let's hope the ice holds long enough for us to steal the potato and get out of here," shivered Hiccup. "That creature would kill us with one snap of its jaws!"

When One Eye finally came to a plunging halt at the ice's edge and Hiccup clambered out of the sleigh, his legs wobbling like jellyfish, the evening had become night. The bright blue road had turned palest turquoise and was gradually fading entirely.

The harbor, thank Thor, was entirely deserted. Pulled up onto the rocks, half-buried in snow, were hundreds of Hysterical boats. Even in their snow-covered state, you could tell these were ghost ships, that hadn't rocked on salt water for fifteen years. Rags of sails hung from drooping masts, oars and rudders jutting from the snow were rotting or snapped in half.

Hiccup sent Toothless off to have a look at the Hysterical Village,

111

and the little dragon reluctantly flapped off into the darkness.

"Why does T-t-toothless always have to do this?" complained Toothless.

"Because you're the one with wings, Toothless," Hiccup explained for the umpteenth time, unhitching One Eye. Camicazi unpacked her burglary equipment, humming happily, shoving interesting-looking pointy instruments into her pockets, putting on her special shoes with spikes on the soles, winding length after length of stout rope around her middle.

Hiccup's usual companion on adventures was Fishlegs, who was always terrified and asking what on earth they were doing in YET ANOTHER life-threatening disaster? So it was quite a change to have Camicazi treating the whole thing as if it were an enjoyable outing.

They put on their skis and waited for Toothless to return from his trip to find out the whereabouts of the Hysterical Village. He gave them a shock when he flapped out from nowhere and landed on Hiccup's shoulder.

"Iss s-s-scary out there," panted Toothless, his eyes glowing luminously in the darkness.

112

"Them Hysterics is having a b-b-banquet for Freya'sday Eve . . . looksa SCRUMMY."

Hiccup explained what Toothless had said to Camicazi, and she got up. "Excellent," she said. "Hopefully they'll be so distracted they won't notice us. Let's get going." The little party set off up the cliff path, One Eye pulling them, his one eye burning bright in the darkness.

9. BACK ON BERK

Back on Berk, Fishlegs was hot as fire, weak as a fly caught in a spider's web, and talking nonsense. Old Wrinkly quietly bathed his head with cool water, and tried to feed him some watery tea.

"Stop it . . . you withered old . . . dried-up crab claw," fretted Fishlegs feebly, trying to twist away from the old man's hand, but hardly strong enough to move.

"They *must* get here before ten in the morning," muttered Old Wrinkly to himself. "He's dying fast."

"Don't worry," whispered Fishlegs, looking straight into Old Wrinkly's concerned old eyes. "Hiccup will make it. Hiccup *always* makes it. . . . Thor only knows how," and then he drifted off into nonsense again.

Out in the middle of the Sullen Sea, strange noises could be heard, like the creaking of an old man's knee, or the rapping of a gigantic knuckle on a door.

The ice was beginning to crack.

Fishlegs was dying fast...

10. FREYA'SDAY EVE ON HYSTERIA

When they reached the top of the cliff, the ground kept on rising up to Mount Hysteria, on which was perched the shadowy outline of the Hysterical Village, all in darkness.

One Eye dragged them right up to the bottom of the village walls, where Camicazi got out her ropes.

She threw up the rope with the metal hook attached, and on the first attempt it caught hold of the top of the wooden wall. She squirmed up it like a little blond monkey and disappeared over the top. One Eye spread wide his wings and flew after her.

Hiccup took a deep breath, grabbed hold of the rope, and climbed up, trying to ignore the skulls grinning at him from the top of the battlements.

They were the only visitors to the Hysterical Village in fifteen years.

The village seemed at first to be deserted.

There was no one in the streets, no light in the windows.

But the Great Hall was blazing with light. Smoke

billowed out of several chimneys, music and chatter and laughing poured out of the windows.

Weirdly, beside the Great Hall, lying on great tree trunks, there stood the largest Viking ship Hiccup had ever seen. It *did* seem a trifle strange to keep a ship so far from the sea, but Hiccup supposed the Hysterics hadn't been doing any sailing at all for the last fifteen years, so perhaps the center of town was as good a place to keep a boat as any.

And what a ship it was . . .

It was more the depth and length of a Roman galleon, and it was the only Viking longboat Hiccup had ever seen with not one but *three* masts. On its prow the figurehead dragon was a snarling Monstrous Nightmare, and Hiccup's heart beat a little faster with excitement as he read the name painted on its side in big flowing letters: *The American Dream*. Perhaps the story Old Wrinkly told him really WAS true . . .

In stark contrast to the ships Hiccup had seen in the harbor, this boat was in tip-top condition. The rest of the village was two meters deep in snow, but *The American*

Dream was spotless, her decks entirely snow-free. She was freshly painted, the Hysterical flag flew cheerily from her central mast and her oars were all out, just as if she were about to set sail for distant shores at a moment's notice.

"We'll climb up onto the roof of the Great Hall and see if we can overhear what's going on," whispered Camicazi. Camicazi didn't even bother to use a rope this time. She just shimmied up the sheer wall, appearing to cling to it with invisible suction like a frog. Once she reached the roof, she let down a rope for Hiccup, and One Eye hauled him up with it.

The roof was thigh deep in snow, and Hiccup had to crawl through it, following the path made by Camicazi. She wriggled through to the central chimney, which had no smoke coming out of it, and she and Hiccup peered down into the room below.

A blast of heat so strong Hiccup had to close his eyes poured out of the chimney. Hiccup's hands burned as they began to warm up. Eventually his watering eyes adjusted to the heat and the light.

Down below, the Hysterics were enjoying a

truly magnificent banquet. The long central table was loaded high with fish, flesh, and fowl cooked in every possible manner, whole stags, entire pigs, and brimming cups of beer and wine. A big drunken guy was dancing a jig on the table at one end, and the Hysterics were laughing and throwing bits of food and napkins at him.

Fires blazed in six huge fireplaces. Enormous white rugs made out of the skin of polar bears were strewn about the floor. Hanging on the walls were the heads of dragons of every possible size, color, and description. And also the heads of a couple of animals Hiccup had never seen before, one that looked like an enormous, depressed deer, and another that resembled a gigantic bull with black, curly hair.

A map of the Barbaric World drawn on deerskin was hanging in a

great curtain against the north wall. On the west of the map, someone had scribbled out the great tumbling waterfall which on most Viking maps was marked "End of the World," and replaced it with a crude charcoal drawing of an island it called AMERICA.

With a sinking of the heart, Hiccup recognized a big blond bearded guy sitting on a throne as the Chief, Norbert the Nutjob. It was definitely the Big Brute who Hiccup had shot with an arrow in the bottom the day before. His throne had a couple of plump cushions on it, but he was shifting from buttock to buttock as if in some pain.

In one hand he held a very unusual, enormous, double-headed axe. The axe was different in that one blade was a bright and shiny copper gold, but the other blade was rusted and blackened, and deeply scarred.

There was no sign of the potato.

Suddenly Hiccup felt a bit foolish. He had somehow expected it to be displayed somewhere obvious, preferably with a big sign underneath it labeling it clearly as THE POTATO.

Because, of course, he did not have any idea what a potato *looked like*, whether it was orange, or

WHAT would a potato look like?
(if such a thing as a potato actually exists)

ould it look like THIS?

how about this?

Or this? Too purple?

sniff sniff

green, or large, or small. Hiccup had somehow imagined it as RED with little black spots, and kind of oblong, or triangular, just because it sounded so exotic. Purple, perhaps? Really, he hadn't a clue.

"OK," whispered Camicazi, "I'm going to have to go down there to try and find out WHERE they keep the potato. . . . It could be absolutely anywhere."

She unwound one of the ropes from around her waist, and Hiccup suggested that they should tie it around One Eye's leg. "That way, if you get into any trouble, you can yank on it three times, and One Eye can haul you up quickly."

One Eye objected strongly to having anything tied around his leg, and only agreed when Hiccup reminded him what a HERO he was going to be in the Dragon World when they returned to Berk with the antidote to Vorpentitis.

The little girl then lowered herself down through the hole in the roof.

It was completely dark and very quiet on top of the Great Hall.

Waiting by the hole, Hiccup felt rather like he had as a small boy going ice fishing with his father, when Stoick cut a hole in the ice, and let down the line, and then all there was to do was wait . . . and wait . . . and wait.

Toothless scratched behind his ears. One Eye picked at his teeth. And Hiccup shivered with anxiety.

"Hurry up, Camicazi . . ."

At any moment Hiccup expected a great crack to appear in that huge flat expanse of frozen sea, and then they would never get home . . . and Fishlegs would be lost.

Or perhaps Camicazi had gotten into trouble down there?

Hiccup peered down through the hole. Camicazi was clinging to her rope like a spider, two meters below them. Hiccup

leaned down a little farther to try and see what was
happening . . .

. . . And then, to his absolute horror, the edge of
the chimney, already buckling under the weight of the
snow, gave way beneath him, and with a shriek, Hiccup
FELL into the Hall.

11. IN THE SOUP

Camicazi watched with round, scared eyes as Hiccup fell past her, arms flailing wildly.

In ordinary circumstances, that would have been the end of Hiccup, for the Great Hall was fully twenty meters high, and he SHOULD have broken his neck falling all the way from the very top.

But, in a series of tremendous strokes of luck, the traditional Freya'sday Eve dish was Onion Soup, and on Hysteria it was served in a truly gigantic cauldron, two meters wide and a meter deep. This pot was sitting on the table directly below the falling Hiccup, and he plunged straight into it, bottom first.

If the soup had been any hotter, Hiccup would have been burned to death, but it had been on the table for some time, and had cooled to a pleasant swimming temperature.

If the Hysterics had been any fonder of Onion Soup, it would not have been deep enough to break Hiccup's fall, but the Hysterics only served Onion Soup because it was the traditional thing to do, and had hardly touched it.

So Hiccup merely bumped his bottom gently on the bottom of the cauldron, and rose to the surface, coughing and spluttering, his hair full of onions. There was a shocked silence. Nothing puts a quicker stop to a jolly meal than a stranger and a great deal of snow suddenly falling onto the banqueting table. The Hysterics sat, amazed, spitting snow out of their beards, staring at the unexpected visitor gasping in their soup.

Norbert the Nutjob was the first to recover, shaking the snow off and leaping to his feet. "ASSASSINS!" he screamed. "SEIZE HIM!"

Twenty Warriors sprang onto the table. Hiccup tried to swim out of trouble, but his backstroke couldn't make up for the fact that he was entirely surrounded. Two large Hysterics dragged him out of the soup and dropped him, dripping and gloopy, in front of Norbert the Nutjob.

"Are there more of you?" barked Norbert the Nutjob, brandishing the blackened blade of his axe in front of Hiccup's face.

Hiccup shook his head, spraying soup in all directions.

Norbert the Nutjob and his Warriors peered upward. Camicazi was hanging way up in the darkness of the ceiling, and her black clothes came in handy, for they could not see her.

"SEARCH THE ROOF AND THE VILLAGE!" screamed Norbert the Nutjob.

He turned to face Hiccup again. Norbert the Nutjob had a tic in his left eye, and it was jerking around frantically like a fly doing a jig.

"I'm sure I recognize you . . . ," he said, using the edge of a nearby Warrior's cloak to wipe the soup off Hiccup's face. "Great Thumbnails of Thor! It's the revolting Hooligan worm who shot an arrow in my Royal Bottom yesterday!"

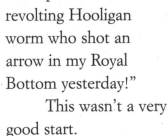

This wasn't a very good start.

"How do you do?" gulped Hiccup politely.

"I DO NOT VERY WELL!"

Norbert the Nutjob

screamed Norbert the Nutjob. "MY BUTTOCKS ARE BURNING!"

The Warriors came panting back into the Hall and said they had searched both the roof and the village, and there were no more Assassins to be found. One Eye and Toothless must have flapped off to hide in the darkness.

Norbert the Nutjob looked rather cross. "You're a very SMALL Assassin," he said huffily, removing Hiccup's sword and stuffing it in his own sword belt. "And so, come to think of it, was the one who attacked us with you yesterday, the one who skied like a grandmother with knee trouble. I know I've been out of the loop for the last fifteen years, but do the Hooligans *really* think they can assassinate me with CHILDREN?"

"I'm *not* an Assassin," pleaded Hiccup quaveringly.

"LIAR!" screeched Norbert the Nutjob, and he lurched forward as if to kill Hiccup with the axe right there and then. And then he calmed himself, and smiled again, and settled himself back on his throne with a wince.

Is THIS a potato? →

"So if you're *not* an Assassin," smiled Norbert, "what are you doing here on Hysteria, shooting me with arrows, and poisoning my soup?"

"I'm looking," said Hiccup, "for THE POTATO."

There was an astonished silence.

"Sssssssh!" said Norbert the Nutjob, looking over his shoulder as if walls had ears. "You're not supposed to NAME the Vegetable-That-No-One-Dares-Name . . ."

"Of course," said Hiccup craftily, "now that I'm *here* I realize that it was all just fairy stories. There's no such thing as a potato, is there? Because there's no such place as America. . . . The earth is as flat as a pancake, and if you sail to the west eventually you just fall off the end of it . . ."

"RUBBISH!" shrieked Norbert the Nutjob. "KILL HIM!" he screamed, his eyes bulging, his mouth foaming, before, with an enormous effort, he gained control of himself again. "No, educate him, *then* kill him!" said Norbert the Nutjob, twiddling his fancy mustaches to soothe himself.

"The earth is as round as a circle, and a circle has no end," explained Norbert carefully. "There *is* such a thing as America, I know because I've been there . . . and as for the Vegetable-That-No-One-Dares-Name . . . I don't know what you're talking about . . ."

"That's because there's no such thing," repeated Hiccup.

"There IS such a thing," insisted Norbert, trying to keep his temper.

"Isn't," said Hiccup.

"Is!"

"Isn't."

"IS!"

"Isn't."

"IS, IS, IS, IS, IS!!!!!" yelled Norbert the Nutjob, twiddling his fancy mustaches so hard they got all tangled in a knot.

"Prove there is," challenged Hiccup.

"I know there's such a thing as a Vegetable-That-No-One-Dares-Name . . . because the Vegetable-That-No-One-Dares-Name . . . *is right here in this room!*" cried

Norbert the Nutjob. He ran over to the
wall where the map of America was
hanging.

With two grand sweeps of his axe he
threw aside the curtain.

"VERY SMALL ASSASSIN," announced
Norbert the Nutjob proudly, "SAY HELLO TO
PAPA . . ."

"Oh whoops!" breathed Hiccup.

Norbert the Nutjob was clearly madder than a
Mad March Hare having a nervous breakdown.

For there, on a stand, larger than life, stood what
looked horribly like the frozen body of Norbert the
Nutjob's Papa.

He was standing proud and upright, every
whisker frozen solid, mouth open in a soundless
YELL, a scary monumental sight. One hand was on his
hip, and in the other he held a casket with glass sides,
filled with ice.

On top of the ice sat the round, rather
disappointing shape of a lumpy brownish vegetable.

Surely THAT can't be the magical, wondrous POTATO,
thought Hiccup. Sticking out of the vegetable was a
single arrow.

Norbert's Papa was surrounded by a carpet of
unusual dragon-creatures, called SQUEALERS.

These weird animals are often used as primitive
burglar-alarm systems. They have no legs to chase after
their prey, so they lie on their backs waving their extra-
long nails gently in the air. Any animal that comes into
contact with those nails causes the whole pack of
Squealers to scream unbearably loudly. The sound is so
piercingly noisy that it actually kills smaller dragons
(who have much better hearing than humans) stone
dead on the spot. The Squealers then devour their
victim, and rather like piranha fish, they can strip
an animal to the bone in sixty seconds flat.

"But, Norbert," gasped Hiccup. "I
thought your father was supposed to be
DEAD?"

"Oh, he's *dead* all right," smiled
Norbert. "He's as dead as a doornail . . .
but as I was keeping the potato frozen
anyway, I thought I'd freeze Papa too."

137

"You *could* give your father a proper Viking funeral," shuddered Hiccup. "He looks untidy standing there . . . and a bit spooky . . ."

"MY FATHER HAS HIS FUNERAL ON THE DAY THE DOOMFANG DIES!" shouted Norbert the Nutjob. "That's why I froze him. Just before my father breathed his last, he stuck into the potato the only arrow he had left given to him by the Feather People, and made me promise to use *this* to get rid of the Doomfang."

"That's impossible," objected Hiccup. "You can't kill a whopping great creature like a Doomfang with *one* tiddly little arrow!"

"Not im-POSSIBLE, weird little red-haired boy," corrected Norbert the Nutjob. "Just im-PROBABLE. And made *more* improbable by the fact that we can't get the arrow OUT of the Vegetable-That-No-One-Dares-Name. . . . Take a look at the inscription on the casket."

Hiccup looked at the casket Bigjob was holding. In it, frozen by the ice, was the disappointingly boring vegetable called the

A Squealer asleep

138

potato. And stuck in this potato was the gaudy little arrow, decorated with brilliant feathers taken from birds Hiccup would not have recognized. American birds that once flew about in undiscovered American skies.

On the front of the casket was written in flowing script the following inscription:

Whomsoever removes the Arrow from this Vegetable Shall Rid Us of the Doomfang and Prove Himself Right True Hero and Ruler of all the Viking Tribes.

"We can't get the arrow OUT of the Precious Vegetable . . ." said Norbert the Nutjob sadly. "We practice all year round with constant arm wrestling, and every year our strongest Champions try and pull it out. Even *I* do not seem to be able to do it, although the verse is obviously referring to ME. The *arrow* is stuck in the vegetable, and *we* are stuck on Hysteria, until the death of my father is avenged."

Hiccup looked at the potato.

"You can't get the arrow out of the potato because it is frozen solid. If you DEFROSTED the potato, a *child* could pull it out," Hiccup suggested.

The tic was back in Norbert the Nutjob's eye.

"My dying father gave me this arrow for a reason," snapped Norbert the Nutjob. "It's supposed to be a test to find out who is strong enough to defeat the Doomfang. What would be the point of the test if just ANYBODY could do it? Who are *you*, anyway, you small boy, and how dare you ask ME all these questions?"

"Now, I'm very glad you brought that up, Norbert," said Hiccup soothingly. "I am Hiccup Horrendous Haddock the Third, only son of Stoick the Vast, and my friend Fishlegs, whom you also met yesterday, has had the Bad Luck to have been bitten by a Venomous Vorpent —"

"That IS Bad Luck," said Norbert the Nutjob with satisfaction. "Certain death, I'd say. I can't say I'm surprised, you know, he seemed like just the sort of little weirdo that Fate would have it in for."

"Fishlegs is not a little weirdo!" interrupted Hiccup. "The point is, Norbert, I have been told that this potato of yours is the only antidote to Vorpent venom, and I wonder if you could possibly spare it to save my friend's life. It would be the kindest thing you've ever done."

Norbert the Nutjob was flabbergasted.

"And what," whispered Norbert the Nutjob, "would you do with my Papa's Precious Vegetable after I gave it to you?"

"Well," said Hiccup, "I guess my friend would eat it."

For a second Norbert the Nutjob stared into space.

Then he was livid with rage, whirling his double-headed axe around his head. "EAT IT????" roared Norbert the Nutjob. "YOU SHOOT ME IN THE BOTTOM AND THEN YOU WANT TO

DIVIDE UP AND EAT MY DEAR DEAD PAPA'S
PRECIOUS AMERICAN VEGETABLE????? KILL
HIM, KILL HIM, KILL HIM!!!!"

After a short struggle, he calmed down again, and
turned to Hiccup with great dignity, holding up his arms.

"I could," said Norbert the Nutjob, "kill you right
now, you Evil Vegetable Murderer . . . but we Hysterics
are not like that. We Hysterics are CIVILIZED. We never
execute before we have given lousy potato-savaging
criminals an absolutely fair trial. And on Hysteria" —
Norbert the Nutjob gave a nasty mad
leer — "the Trial you face is
Trial by Axe."

Oh, crumbs,
thought Hiccup.

Norbert the Nutjob
strode over to the middle of the
room where there was a large tree trunk,
lopped off at the base.

"Fate herself shall decide your Fate," said
Norbert the Nutjob. "I shall throw my axe high into
the air . . . and if it lands with the golden side burying
itself into the wood, I shall allow you to live. But if it
lands on the dark side" — Norbert the Nutjob stroked

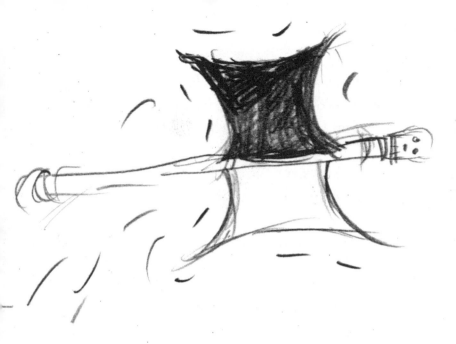

the dark side lovingly — "if it lands on the *dark* side, I shall kill you with this very axe, on the spot. I hope you're feeling lucky . . ."

Norbert stepped back dramatically. He gazed up at the heavens . . .

"COME, GREAT POWERS OF FATE AND DESTINY," yelled Norbert the Nutjob. "I SWEAR TO DO AS YOU TELL ME. LIFE OR DEATH?"

The axe soared toward the ceiling, spinning slowly through the air. It began to fall, first the bright side down, then the dark.

Hiccup was not as tough as the other boys, but his

eyesight was very good. He could see the axe was going to land dark side down, and he leaped in between the dark and bright blades, and caught the axe with its wooden handle just before the dark side landed in the wood.

The Hysterics gasped.

High up on a beam in the ceiling, Camicazi gasped too.

Hiccup heaved the axe above his head and drove the bright blade deep into the tree trunk.

"BRIGHT SIDE WINS, NORBERT THE NUTJOB," shouted Hiccup Horrendous Haddock the Third, his hands on his hips.

Nobody knew quite what to do.

Norbert the Nutjob's mouth opened and shut like a fish out of water.

"You CHEATED!" screamed Norbert the Nutjob.

"Fate must have *let* me cheat," Hiccup pointed out. "Now set me free like you promised."

Norbert looked as if he was about to explode. He was used to terrified adults who cowered down before him and his terrible Axe of Fate.

He WASN'T used to bossy small boys who told him to defrost his Precious Potato and bury his Papa, and who caught his Axe before it landed.

But what if Hiccup was right, and Fate had really meant to LET Hiccup cheat?

Norbert did not dare annoy FATE herself.

"SEIZE HIM!" screamed Norbert. "He can live, but he can live out his days in prison! *That* will teach him to shoot arrows at NORBERT THE NUTJOB!"

Four or five burly Hysterics grabbed Hiccup and dragged him to a small cage suspended by a single chain from a beam in the rafters above. They pushed him in and locked the cage, returning the key to Norbert, who put it in his pocket.

And then the Hysterics forgot about Hiccup, and partied long, long into the night, laughing and singing and eating and drinking too much.

Hiccup sat silently in the small cage, trying to think of a Cunning Plan to get out of *this* situation.

It didn't look too good.

Even if he *could* escape from the locked cage, steal the potato and get away without a single Hysteric noticing, he could hear some ominous creaking noises coming from the ice outside. . . . Loud crackings and knockings, like the striking of an enormous sword upon a stone.

The ice was beginning to melt, and once the

Doomfang was free again there would be no way out of Hysteria . . .

As the long night wore on, one by one the Hysterics fell asleep in their chairs or on the floor, or, in the case of one fat Warrior, on top of the table hugging the remains of the roasted boar. Norbert the Nutjob slumbered on his throne, his thumb in his mouth, cradling his double-headed axe. High up in the ceiling of the Great Hall Camicazi was sleeping, clinging to her beam like a little black cat. Time ticked on, and Hiccup struggled to keep awake, but eventually the gentle rocking of the cage, and the cloudy heat and fumes of alcohol in the room overpowered him, and he too nodded off.

146

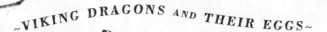

SQUEALERS

Squealers are strange
blobby, sluglike creatures
who are so lazy they have
developed an interesting
method of stunning their prey with a single
shriek. A pack of Squealers can strip their
victim to the bone quicker than a shoal of
piranha fish.

~STATISTICS~

COLORS: Slug black.
ARMED WITH: Scream so loud it can
knock a smaller dragon unconscious.
Piranha-like jaws and fangs... 8
POISON: None...... 0
HUNTING ABILITY: ... 7
SPEED: Hardly move at all..... 0
**FEAR AND FIGHT
FACTOR:** Scary if you are
wounded or are on the
small side.... 7

12. WILL TOOTHLESS SAVE THE DAY?

Meanwhile, up on the roof, Toothless and One Eye had flapped off and hidden in *The American Dream* when they heard the noise of Hiccup falling into the Onion Soup, and the Hysteric Warriors charging outside to look for other Assassins.

When things grew quiet again, they flew back to the chimney. Both dragons were cold, hungry, and tired. One Eye's eye gleamed golden-yellow in the darkness.

"Shall we leave them?" One Eye mused to himself. "It looks like they haven't found the cure for Vorpentitis after all . . . and I'm not hanging around here just to save the skin of a couple of stinking Humans . . ."

"S-s-selfish Humans!" grumbled Toothless. "They n-n-never think of poor, cold H-H-H-HUNGRY Toothless!"

One Eye snorted. "Well, I don't blame them for that. You're

just a lap-dragon, an overgrown rat. And YOU shouldn't be hungry anyway. Who ate all the snacks in the sleigh on the way here, I'd like to know?"

". . . I'll give them till morning," One Eye decided, letting the rope attached to his leg flop down the chimney and into the Great Hall again, and settling himself in the snow to sleep on the roof. "My aunt Snaggletooth died of Vorpentitis, and it's a nasty way to go."

"Toothless not s-s-sleeping here!" moaned Toothless, outraged. "Iss too cold! Toothless D-D-DELICATE, sensitive . . ." He checked whether the big dragon was really asleep. One Eye gave a deep rumbling snore and Toothless carried on, ". . . not like YOU, you big, white, gormless mountain gorilla . . ."

One Eye's one eye snapped open, and his big Saber-Toothed jaws lashed out toward Toothless . . . but they shut on thin air, for Toothless had the reflexes of a bluebottle, and he had already tumbled down through the hole in the roof. Toothless soared into the Great Hall, over the

heads of the sleeping, mumbling
Hysterics, and landed on top of Hiccup's
cage. The cage swung violently to the right,
and Hiccup's head banged sharply on one
of the bars, waking him up.

"Ow!" protested Hiccup,
looking straight into the upside-
down greengage eyes of his pet dragon.

"Toothless!" he whispered joyfully.

"Thank Thor you're here; you see how right I
was to bring you -- you can save the day!"

"HA!" grunted Toothless crossly.

"Just flap over to that big frozen Viking over
there, will you, and steal the potato, and then we'll
be off . . ." whispered Hiccup.

Toothless looked where Hiccup was pointing, to
Norbert's Papa, Bigjob, and the casket, and gave a
shriek of terror.

"S-s-squealers!" he gasped, and jumped into the
cage, burying his face in Hiccup's leg.

"Oh, goodness, yes, I'd forgotten. Squealers
can kill a dragon as small as you, can't they?"
remembered Hiccup, soothing the little dragon by

151

stroking him on the back. "OK, don't steal the potato, but the key to this cage is in Norbert the Nutjob's pocket, and if you could just flap off and get it . . ."

But Toothless had smelled the Onion Soup on Hiccup's leg, and he gave it a lick.

"Onion S-s-soup!" said Toothless accusingly. "You bin eating Onion S-s-soup!"

"Yes, yes," said Hiccup hurriedly, "I fell in the soup, but about the key —"

But this was the last straw as far as Toothless was concerned. He was FURIOUS, and he swelled up to nearly twice his size with anger, and flew out of the cage like an infuriated little balloon.

"SNOT fair! SNOT fair!" snorted Toothless. "You been stuffing yourself with Onion S-s-soup and poor T-t-toothless STARVING and now you want Toothless to f-f-face a whole load of Squealers with no food in his t-t-tummy? TYPICAL! Well, you can just WAIT, that's all. . . . Toothless'll have his supper and THEN maybe he'll help you out . . ."

"TOOTHLESS!" whispered Hiccup, as loud as he dared, "THIS IS IMPORTANT! GET THAT KEY RIGHT NOW OR I'LL . . . I'LL . . . I'LL . . ."

"You'll what?" jeered Toothless cheekily, flapping out of Hiccup's way as he desperately tried to grab Toothless's tail through the bars of the cage.

Sticking out his little pink forked tongue, Toothless hopped down onto the banqueting tables and tucked into the roast buffalo pie, ignoring Hiccup's furious, frustrated whispers from the cage swinging a couple of meters above.

"Toothless can't hear!" sang Toothless through a mouthful of pumpkin. "Got s-s-something in his ear! Oooooh, that rhymes. . . . Toothless ca-a-an't he-ar, got something in his e-ar! Toothless ca-a-an't he-ar, got something in his e-ar!"

And for the next five minutes, Toothless pretended to be quite deaf, and took his time hopping from plate to plate, gorging himself on

153

deep-fried mackerel, turkey wings, and sweetcorn fritters.

Eventually, he swallowed the last remains of the pie, took a big swig of the Homemade Nettle Champagne, burped, and rubbed his stomach contentedly.

"That's b-b-better. Toothless can hear now. Wossat you saying?"

"WILL YOU GET THAT KEY FROM NORBERT THE NUTJOB'S POCKET BEFORE HE MURDERS US?" hissed Hiccup at the top of his whisper.

"S-s-say pretty please . . . ," sang Toothless.

"Pretty please," whispered Hiccup through gritted teeth.

"OK, OK, keep your hair on," said Toothless, and he took off (rather wobbly, because he had eaten so much), and crashlanded on Norbert the Nutjob's chest. Luckily, Norbert was so dead to the world he merely grunted, and hugged his axe a little closer.

Giggling, Toothless snipped off both of Norbert the Nutjob's fancy mustaches with two bites of his sharp little gums, and then he staggered into Norbert's pocket and pulled out the key.

Toothless
marched across
the banqueting table
with the key in his mouth,
spitting it out every now and
then to make pointed remarks to Hiccup.

"Is TYPICAL," snorted Toothless. "T-t-typical.
Poor old starving T-t-toothless, woken up from his
H-h-hibernation Nap just to save the day YET
AGAIN."

Toothless put the key back in his mouth, and this
time, his large, overfull belly prevented him from seeing
exactly where he was putting his feet, and he tripped
over a knife lying in the middle of the table.

Toothless lurched forward, knocking a candle off
the table and onto the floor, where it promptly set fire
to a polar bear rug. He did a couple of somersaults,
spinning over and over until he landed bottom first in
the wild boar stew, and . . . swallowed the key.

"G-g-gulp . . . ," said Toothless.

gulp

Gulp

13. THE GREAT POTATO BURGLARY

"AAAARGH!" raged Hiccup, shaking the bars of his cage. "Typical! Five minutes ago I was just locked in a cage in a room full of Hysteric Warriors. NOW you've swallowed the key and set fire to the room! Flap up and wake up Camicazi and then PUT OUT THAT FIRE!"

"S-s-say pretty please . . . ," choked Toothless defiantly.

"PRETTY PLEASE!" howled Hiccup in the loudest whisper he could whisper.

Toothless flew unsteadily up to the beam where Camicazi was sleeping, and woke her up by shrieking softly, "No key! No key!" in her ear, before flying back to deal with the fire.

Camicazi took charge of the situation from the moment she opened her eyes. She got up, calmly balancing on the beam, for all the world as if she was safely down on the ground rather than almost twenty meters up in the air.

She unwound another rope from around her

waist, and threw the metal end of it so that it wrapped around the beam from which Hiccup's cage was suspended. She pulled to check it was secure, and then swung out, clinging to the rope, and landed on the top of Hiccup's cage.

Camicazi wriggled down the outside of the cage, and looked hard at the lock on the door. She felt in her pocket and brought out a long pinlike instrument, and stuck it in the lock, wiggling it expertly from side to side.

"That was *so* brave of you!" she whispered. "For a *boy*, of course. . . . Leaping down into the soup like that! We'd NEVER have found out where they kept the potato if you hadn't done that . . ."

Hiccup considered telling her it had all been a total accident, and then thought better of it. "Oh, you know . . . ," he whispered modestly back. "It was nothing. I do that kind of . . . *leaping* all the time. What are you doing?"

"Picking the lock," replied Camicazi airily. "Locks are nothing to us Bog-Burglars . . . no prisons can hold us. We're as wriggly as eels. We're as jumpy as crickets."

The lock suddenly clicked loudly, and the door of Hiccup's cage swung open.

"Your exit, my lord," grinned Camicazi.

Hiccup scrambled out of the cage, and dropped down onto the banqueting table below, unable to believe his luck.

"And *now*," frowned Camicazi, "for the Vegetable-That-No-One-Dares-Name. We haven't got a lot of time."

Indeed they hadn't.

Toothless had tried to snuff out the fire on the polar bear rug by smothering it with his wings, and when that didn't work, he threw Homemade Nettle Champagne on it.

The flames sprang up a meter high and the fire spread to a nearby chair.

"Oh d-d-dear!" wailed Toothless. "Toothless m-m-messed up . . . all Toothless's fault . . . ohdearohdear . . ."

"Toothless," Hiccup ordered, "stop making that fire WORSE and come over here. We're going to need YOUR help to steal the potato."

Toothless flapped over, his guilt making him unexpectedly obedient.

"I want you to melt the ice in the casket," said Hiccup.

"B-b-but the Squealers?" whimpered Toothless.

Hiccup wound his scarf around the little dragon's ears, to act as earplugs.

"Wait until Toothless has finished melting the ice, just in case you DO set off the Squealers," he explained to Camicazi. "The sound could STUN a dragon as titchy as Toothless if he's too close."

"T-t-titchy?" huffed Toothless. "Toothless not like the word TITCHY."

"You're looking at the burglary EXPERT," said Camicazi. "There's *no way* I'm going to set off those Squealers."

By some miracle, all the Hysterics were so dead to the world that not even all this noise and commotion, and a large fire blazing in the middle of their Great Hall, had woken them up. They snored on, oblivious.

Trembling with terror (and flying rather erratically because he was weighed down by his fur coat, his large meal, and the scarf around his head that was slipping over his eyes), Toothless flew over the waving nails of the Squealers. This was very brave of him, for if he looked down he could see their horrible black bodies with the piranha teeth, and to a dragon as

Toothless with Hiccup's scarf wound around his head, to act as earplugs.

small as Toothless, it was like wandering casually in front of a pack of lions with open jaws.

Hovering above the casket, he was so scared that for a moment his fireholes seized up, and he couldn't breathe out a single flame, only clouds and clouds of bluey-grey smoke.

"Relax ...," whispered Hiccup from the table. "Breathe deeply ... no pressure ... you've got all the time in the world ..." Hiccup was trying to sound as calm as he could even though half the room was on fire.

"All the time in the world . . . ," sang Hiccup nervously. "Just relax . . . go to your happy place . . ."

The nails of the Squealers began to twitch as they sensed the smoke.

"HA!" puffed Toothless furiously, practically disappearing he was making so much steam.

"Toothless's h-h-happy place! Happy place N-N-NOT here!" And to Hiccup's intense relief, Toothless's final indignant snort ended in a big breath of fire that engulfed the entire casket.

"Don't set fire to the potato!" Hiccup reminded him.

"S-s-set fire to this! DON'T set fire to that!" complained Toothless. "Mister Hiccup just stop being such a B-BOSSY-BOOTS and give a dragon a chance!"

But he made his flame smaller, and directed it steadily at the ice around the potato, and slowly, surely, the ice began to melt.

Meanwhile, Camicazi climbed back up to the ceiling again, and wriggled along the beams until she was directly above Norbert's Papa.

She let herself down on another rope, so that she was hanging, like a little spider, about a meter above

the casket, and then she wound the rope around her ankle and flipped upside down.

She waited until Toothless had finished melting the ice, and had flapped off back to the safe distance of Hiccup's shoulder.

Right in front of Norbert's Papa's frozen staring eyes, Camicazi reached into the casket and carefully, delicately, removed the potato with the arrow stuck in it from the bed of ice.

Hiccup held his breath. If the casket *was* booby-trapped, *this* would be the moment that something might happen . . .

But there did not seem to be any booby traps.

Camicazi swung there, potato in one hand. Norbert's Papa wobbled for a second on his stand, but he was still grinning ferociously, his eyes staring straight ahead at nothing. (He was DEAD, after all.) The snores of the sleeping Hysterics rumbled peacefully through the quiet Hall.

Camicazi put the potato in her pocket.

"She's done it, she's done it, she's done it . . . ," whispered Hiccup to himself.

Camicazi was about to turn herself the right way

up again and climb the rope, but then she spotted something else in the casket.

"Uh oh . . . ," whispered Hiccup.

Camicazi couldn't resist. She reached in and picked the something else out of the casket . . .

For one second it seemed like it still might be all right again.

But it turned out that the frozen body of Norbert's Papa was very carefully balanced, and when this second weight was removed from the casket, it began to tip s-l-o-w-l-y backward, and then gathering speed, until the entire body crashed like a great tree trunk into the waving forest of Squealers down below.

166

screeched the Squealers.

The noise they made was simply earsplitting.

The glass of the frozen casket shattered into pieces, and the ice inside fell to the floor.

All over the room, the Hysterics sat bolt upright as if electrified, blearily opening their eyes and saying "Wossat? Wassgoing on?" to each other. Even with the scarf *and* Hiccup's hands over his ears, poor old Toothless nearly fainted from the loudness of the noise.

"Watch out, Camicazi!" yelled Hiccup. Norbert the Nutjob woke up, and threw his double-headed axe straight at Camicazi, dangling from her rope. Camicazi saw the axe coming, and let herself drop.

The axe missed, and Camicazi landed on the floor, or, more precisely, on the gigantic wobbly stomach of a Hysteric who was so dead to the world he didn't even wake up.

Norbert the Nutjob ran to drag his frozen father out of the mass of shrieking Squealers. Stiff and ice-cold as he was, they still tried to eat him, blunting their teeth on his hard frozen legs, slashing their horrible long nails on his solid-frozen mustaches. Once he had pulled his Papa to safety, the Squealers stopped screaming as abruptly as they had begun. Norbert the Nutjob drew his sword and strode toward Camicazi, with a murderous expression on his face . . .

"GET OUT OF HERE!" screamed Camicazi. "I'll be all right; don't worry about me!"

Hiccup was standing right in the middle of the table. About twenty large Warriors were already advancing toward him, swords, axes, and daggers drawn. The odds were not on Hiccup's side . . . and Hiccup was completely and entirely unarmed.

He had no bow and arrow, no dagger. He did not even have his sword, for Norbert the Nutjob had taken it from him earlier, if you remember. (Which was a shame, because Hiccup was good at sword-fighting.)

So, in absence of his sword, Hiccup picked up two large, sloppy, creamy pumpkin pies, and crashed them like cymbals on either side of another Warrior's face. The Hysteric fell backward, a sticky, dripping,

pumpkin mess, and promptly sat down on the smaller Warrior behind him.

Meanwhile, dodging Hysteric sword-thrusts, Hiccup grabbed the nearest thing to hand, which happened to be a gigantic half-eaten TURKEY carcass, and shoved it over the head of the closest Warrior. The Hysteric's arms were pinned by his sides; muffled shouting noises came from within the turkey; and he staggered off, like a grotesquely large dead chicken with human legs.

Hiccup was getting into the swing of things. He tipped an entire bowl of maple syrup on the floor, sending the Hysterics slipping and sliding all over the place. He winded another Warrior with a watermelon.

He pelted them all with onions. Now that the Squealers had stopped squealing, Toothless flew down from the roof to join in the battle. He found a bowl of chestnuts, sucked up a whole mouthful so that his cheeks were bulging like a hamster, and zoomed over the heads of the Warriors, spitting out fire and red-hot roasted chestnuts like a barrage of flaming bullets.

Chaos reigned in the Great Hall. Vegetables flew in all directions. Hysterics who had been woken by a

fat overripe tomato splattered in their faces assumed that this was all just a merry midnight food fight, and enthusiastically attacked their fellow Hysterics.

"Hurry up, Camicazi!" screamed Hiccup, slapping another opponent around the cheek with a large flat flounder, and running up the other end of the table.

Camicazi had problems of her own. She was defending herself against Norbert the Nutjob, who was livid with rage and lashing out at her with his sword.

Norbert the Nutjob had had a trying couple of days. His bottom was still throbbing from the arrow wound, Hiccup had made a fool out of him in the Ordeal-by-Axe, somebody appeared to have bitten off his beloved mustaches, and the Hooligans were even now stealing his Papa's American Vegetable.

And they hadn't even had the decency to send some proper adult Assassins! This third Assassin was even smaller than the first two. To add insult to injury, he, Norbert the Nutjob, noble Chief of the Hysteric Tribe, and Master Swordsman, was finding it difficult to defeat this *tiny little blond Assassin* in one-to-one combat. She just wouldn't stay still.

She met every lunge he made, carelessly singing

the Bog-Burglar national
anthem as she did so. She
performed cartwheels between
moves. She even picked up a
piece of wild boar sandwich off
the floor and started to eat it,
while still fighting.

She talked
CONSTANTLY.

"I hope you don't

mind me eating on the job," she said chattily, easily deflecting his Grimbeard's Grapple sword-thrust, and throwing in a Piercing Point of her own. "I know it's rather rude to fight with my mouth full, but I'm absolutely STARVING, haven't eaten a thing all evening . . ."

Norbert the Nutjob gave a grim smile and sprang forward with a particularly violent sword-thrust.

She dodged it, leapt up, swung on his beard while she wiped her sticky fingers on his shirt-front, and sprang back down again.

"I'm going to KILL you . . ." panted Norbert the Nutjob, his eyes watering with the pain of having his beard pulled. "First with my sword, and then with my axe, and then I'm going to feed you to the Squealers."

"You clever, *clever* boy!" sang Camicazi, delightedly spotting her rope dangling just behind his head. "But you'll have to CATCH me first, you know . . ."

And with that, she somersaulted right between his legs, came up the other side, and squirmed up her rope with astonishing speed, pulling the end of it up behind her.

Norbert the Nutjob looked down at his legs for a dazed moment, and then through them, and then he swung around to find that Camicazi had apparently vanished into thin air.

He whirled around again. She wasn't there either. How *completely extraordinary* . . .

Camicazi, swinging centimeters above Norbert the Nutjob's head, removed his crown so gently, *so* softly, with her pickpocketing, burglaring fingers, that he never felt a thing.

She then bashed him on the head as hard as she could with the frozen potato.

Norbert staggered a bit, swayed this way and that, and then fell to the floor, unconscious. As he lay prone, Camicazi dropped back down to the ground again and patted him reassuringly on the shoulders.

"Practice, Norbert, that's what you need," she said condescendingly. "You're never too old to learn."

"CAMICAZI!!!!!" shrieked Hiccup from the banqueting table, knocking out a Hysteric with a leg of roasted buffalo, shoving a carrot up the nose of another, and spraying three more with Homemade Nettle Champagne. "GET OVER HERE!" Camicazi swung across and landed on the table beside him.

Most of the table was now in flames, and the fire had spread to ALL the polar bear rugs.

Most ominous of all, the Squealers were actually MOVING to get out of the Hall. Squealers are so lazy that they only move when they are in mortal danger. They wriggled toward the door like disgusting fat, bloated slugs, their nails waving frantically, leaving a trail of snotty slime.

The rope that snaked up to the chimney in the ceiling, the other end of which was attached to One Eye's great leg, dangled between Camicazi and Hiccup.

They both grabbed hold of it, coughing from the smoke, and tugged three times.

Just the second before One Eye dragged them up and out of danger, Hiccup leaned down and picked up a metal food tray from the table.

And then they were up and away, the Hysteric swords just brushing their heels as they rose swiftly to the ceiling and out through the hole in the roof.

14. THE POTATO-BURGLARS' RUN

They appeared, blinking like moles, into the daylight, for night had turned into morning while they were in the Hysterical Great Hall; the sky was no longer black but the bluey-grey of a seagull's back, and the sun was coming up fast from behind the Mazy Multitudes.

Down below they could hear the roar of the Hysterics, the loudest of all being Norbert the Nutjob shouting, "MY VEGETABLE! THEY'VE GOT MY VEGETABLE!"

The Hysterics were already stampeding toward the door, in pursuit.

Hiccup knew they hadn't a hope of getting away on foot, and they didn't have time to find their skis again.

In such situations, being tough is not necessarily the way to stay alive, because *however* tough you are, if there are five hundred Hysterics on skis and only FOUR of you, you are not going to win the battle.

What you need in THIS kind of situation is a

Clever Idea, and luckily Hiccup was good at Clever
Ideas.

Hiccup put the food tray down on the roof and
sat on it.

"Come on, Camicazi, you sit behind me,"
ordered Hiccup.

"Oh, goody," said Camicazi, her eyes lighting up.

The roof of the Great Hall hung slightly over the
village walls. From there a steep slope ran all the way
down to the harbor.

So when the Hysterics poured out of the doors
of the Great Hall in a shouting, angry river they had an
excellent view of Camicazi and Hiccup tobogganing

down the roof and sailing over the walls of the village on board one of their silver food trays.

"AAAAIEEEEEEEEEE!!!!!!!!!!!!" screamed Hiccup and Camicazi as they soared through the air.

By some miracle they landed the right way up on the slope below.

And then the lightning descent began.

Take it from me, there is nothing on earth that moves faster than two children going down a practically vertical slope on a highly polished silver food tray.

Hiccup had sledded before, but never on a hill so steep that it was practically a cliff. And in fact the exact

179

descent that they made has now become an annual competition on Hysteria. It is known as the Potato-Burglars' Run, and it follows the same route that Hiccup and Camicazi took, starting, as they did, on top of the roof of the Great Hall, and ending, less than two minutes later, in Hysteria Harbor.

The Potato-Burglars' Run is the most dangerous toboggan run in the Inner Isles, and for those brave enough to try it, accidents are common.

Hiccup and Camicazi were lucky not to break their necks. They screamed down that hillside, wildly out of control, yelling at the tops of their voices.

One Eye and Toothless couldn't possibly keep up with them, for it was like trying to catch a speeding arrow.

When they hit the ice of the harbor two bottom-bruising, hair-raising, eye-popping minutes later, they were going so fast that they wildly overshot the sleigh they had left there, and *The Hopeful Puffin* patiently waiting for their return.

They scrambled off the food tray and raced toward the sleigh. One Eye came soaring down, and they hurriedly hitched him up and set him going at a brisk trot toward the Harbor Exit.

"Oh my goodness," panted Camicazi, looking

back up at the Hysterical Village, where the Great Hall was now a gigantic bonfire. "Those Hysterics are going to be SO CROSS."

"My congratulations," growled One Eye to Hiccup, as he pulled them rapidly forward. "You are the first Human I have ever met who uses his brain and not just his muscles."

"If he really use his b-b-brain," complained Toothless, catching up and collapsing, exhausted, on the seat of the sleigh, "we not here in the first p-p-place."

In that very same instant, over the brow of the hill came the Hysterics.

They had put their helmets on and they were on skis, howling the Hysterical Howl like a pack of speeding wolves. They were already shooting arrows in their direction, trying to hit the sleigh. But they were too late. Once their skis hit the ice they traveled for a while, and then came to a halt. Hiccup and Camicazi were nearly at the Harbor Exit by now, and the arrows shot by the Hysterics fell harmlessly on the ice.

Looking over her shoulder at the furious Hysterics, Camicazi let out a whoop of joy as One Eye galloped out of Hysteria Harbor.

"We made it!" she yelled.

"We haven't made it *yet*," said Hiccup nervously. That sharp noise of cracking, like axes on a tree trunk, was even louder now that they were on the ice. And Hiccup was looking out for the Doomfang.

"Here's the Vegetable," said Camicazi, handing Hiccup the Frozen Potato with the arrow stuck in it. "And this other thing I found in the casket — I'm sorry, I shouldn't have taken it as well, but once you start burgling, it's difficult to stop."

Hiccup took the Potato and the Other Thing, and stuffed them in his breast pocket, not really concentrating, for the great shadow of the Doomfang had appeared under the boat, and was following them under the ice.

"If we can *just* get to the Open Sea before the ice cracks we'll be all right," muttered Hiccup to himself. "The Doomfang won't leave the Wrath of Thor. The Doomfang hasn't left the Wrath of Thor in fifteen years . . ."

The walls of the cliffs raced past them on either side. The Doomfang, dark and terrible, stretching out forever, swam slowly beneath them. And they reached the edge of the Open Sea without the ice cracking.

"You see!" grinned Camicazi. "We *did* it!"

15. THEY MIGHT JUST MAKE IT, NOW

It seemed like they had INDEED done it, as they burst into the Open Sea, One Eye pulling into that Great White Wilderness at terrific speed, the Wrath of Thor left behind them, the potato safely in Hiccup's breast pocket, and Berk only a three-hour sleigh ride away.

And then everything went wrong.

"What's th-th-that???" stammered Toothless, pointing with one wing to a shape on the ice behind them, coming closer by the second.

That was an enormous, leaping Driver Dragon, far bigger and faster than One Eye, pulling a gigantic sleigh with one man in it. A very *cross* man, with an arrow wound in his bottom, a lump on his head, chewed-off mustaches, and a double-headed axe in one hand.

In fact it was Norbert the Nutjob.

Before Hiccup had time to think, Norbert was upon them.

His sleigh drew alongside the galloping One Eye. And then he reached over, and with one blow of his axe, he cut the reins and tackle attaching One Eye to the sleigh.

One Eye bounded on, but the sleigh, and *The Hopeful Puffin* behind it, came to a shuddering halt.

"Oh, *suffering scallops*," moaned Hiccup.

There they were, as still as a stone, in the middle of a Great White Desert that stretched for miles and miles and miles. In front of them, Norbert the Nutjob was pulling on his Saber-Tooth's reins to wheel his sleigh around for the attack.

Below them was the Doomfang.

For the first time in fifteen years, the Doomfang had left the Wrath of Thor.

It, too, had stopped when the sleigh stopped. In fact the sleigh had come to rest right in the center of its terrible green eye, as if it were a target.

And a target it was, for Norbert the Nutjob.

Norbert leaped into their sleigh, tall and terrible and COMPLETELY CRAZY.

"AHA!" roared Norbert the Nutjob, his tic dancing for pure horrible murderous joy. "I'VE CAUGHT YOU, YOU REVOLTING LITTLE BLOND ASSASSIN! AND NOW I SHALL TEACH YOU NOT TO HIT PEOPLE ON THE HEAD WITH THEIR OWN VEGETABLE!"

Norbert the Nutjob raised his axe over Camicazi, and he was about to bring it down, when Hiccup said loudly, "I wouldn't do that, Norbert."

Hiccup felt in his breast pocket, and drew out the potato with the arrow still stuck in it. It was warmer this morning, and the potato, snuggled down the front of Hiccup's furry waistcoat, was no longer frozen.

Norbert glanced at Hiccup, and then gasped in astonishment, as right in front of Norbert's eyes . . .

. . . HICCUP PULLED THE ARROW OUT OF THE POTATO.

For as Hiccup had suggested earlier to Norbert, the arrow slid out perfectly easily now that the potato had defrosted.

Hiccup pushed it in and out of the

potato several times just to drive the point home.

Norbert the Nutjob dropped his axe.

"My father's Prophecy!" screamed Norbert the Nutjob, his head in his hands. "I don't believe it. . . . It can't be true! You . . . you revolting little Hooligan Vegetable-Burglar . . . *you* . . . are the Chosen One? . . . *You* will lift the Curse and rid us of the Doomfang . . . ?"

Hiccup nodded solemnly, thinking, *nutty as a fruitcake*.

At that very moment, the sun came over the horizon . . .

Rays of sunlight bounced off the snow and ice all around them, and off the Doomfang's Great Green Eye and dazzled Hiccup, so that he had to fling up an elbow to shield himself from the glare.

A sound like a million whips rang out, or a trillion axe blows, or a thousand of Thor's thunderbolts rolled into one.

The ice cracked from side to side.

16. THE DOOMFANG

A great jagged split appeared in the white frozen sea, a split that ran all the way from the Outcast Lands to the north, down to the Bog-Burglar islands in the south.

The world broke open like a big white egg.

"Aaaaaargh!" screamed Hiccup. "Quick! Get into *The Hopeful Puffin*!"

Norbert the Nutjob, Camicazi, and Hiccup bolted out of the sleigh, and leaped into the little boat, the ice giving way beneath their feet.

"LET DOWN THE SAIL!" screamed Hiccup, cutting the rope tying the boat to the sleigh.

The sail flopped down and the wind caught it, sending it billowing outward like a plump cushion. There was another enormous **CRACK!** and the ice in the Sullen Sea splintered into millions of tiny pieces.

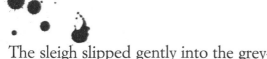

The sleigh slipped gently into the grey-green water and was seen no more, and *The Hopeful Puffin* was afloat.

Through the jagged jigsaw of ice, between them and the Isle of Berk on the horizon, up rose the Doomfang.

It reared out of the sea, showering *The Hopeful Puffin* with water and shards of ice, telescoping upward to its immense height, which was impossibly, RIDICULOUSLY high, blotting out the newly risen sun.

The SOUND it made was unutterably awful, a sadness so extreme it made you want to weep yourself, a sound that crept up the spine like spiders' feet, and scuttled over the scalp, sending each individual hair on Hiccup's head prickling upward like the spines on a hedgehog. It was the glossy black of a gigantic, muscly panther, and when it opened its awful Cavern jaws to roar, its serrated teeth were as green as its eyes, and the yellow frothy scum of its saliva steamed and smoked in the cold morning air.

Indeed, its whole body seemed boiling hot, and like the flanks of a horse that has galloped for miles, great clouds of smoke rose up from its tremendous gleaming bulk and into the sky.

"It's come for *me* . . . ," moaned Norbert the Nutjob, in a tremble of fear.

"No, it hasn't," said Hiccup. "It's come for ME."

And the Doomfang *did* seem to be looking directly down at Hiccup.

It was as if Hiccup had always known that this was going to happen, that somehow he was *never* going to get in and out of Hysteria without meeting the Doomfang face-to-face.

"Don't look into its eyes," warned One Eye.

You should never look into a dragon's eyes. But in this case it was difficult *not* to — they were so large and so close, like a couple of green suns. Hiccup was hypnotized for a moment, and his head spun so that he nearly lost his balance and dropped off the boat.

"What do you WANT?" Hiccup yelled desperately in Dragonese.

The Dragon opened its great mouth and tried to speak. But all that came out was a terrible unearthly howl of horror and SADNESS, and the foam dripped from its jaws in a revolting bubbly waterfall. It tried again, and the terrible sound came out again, only louder.

"What is it?" asked Hiccup.

But the creature could not say, and its struggle to speak made it angry, and it began shooting out with its blue flames, nearer and nearer to Hiccup. "What does it want me to *do*?" asked Hiccup frantically.

"We're done for," despaired Norbert, wringing his hands.

Camicazi patted the moaning Norbert soothingly on the back. "We'll be all right," she repeated over and over again, "we always are, Thor only knows how. . . . Hiccup'll have a Cunning Plan . . ."

"Oh that's right," remembered Norbert. "Of course! My father's Prophecy! *He* is the Chosen One, and he alone can rid us of the Doomfang!"

But for once in his life, Hiccup did NOT have a Cunning Plan.

"What do you want?" asked Hiccup again, more to himself, this time.

The Doomfang made one last terrible attempt to communicate, coming out with a truly dreadful, garbled cacophony of noise, and then opened its jaws wide, sucking in its breath.

Hiccup did not know what they had done for the creature to have it in for them.

Perhaps it had gone crazy and turned into a Man-Eater? It had certainly killed Norbert's Papa, fifteen years ago, and was it now going to kill *them* too?

Because now it was aiming directly for them, and Hiccup braced himself for the Monster to breathe out its flames and set the boat alight like a little barbecue.

But what shot out of the creature's mouth was not a Terrible Burst of Fire, not the frozen flames that would have sent all three of them, and Toothless too, straight to Valhalla in a heroic bonfire.

Curling and unfurling, quick and flexible as a gigantic muscly snake, out of the Doomfang's mouth came the Doomfang's TONGUE.

One hundred meters long, pink and pulsing, the Doomfang's TONGUE sped straight to Hiccup's left hand, and the wriggling, squirming, revoltingly WET forked end of it burrowed its way into his palm and wrapped itself around the potato.

Hiccup nearly dropped the potato there and then. But then he realized what the creature wanted.

He dropped the arrow, and grabbed hold of the potato with both hands. The juices of the Doomfang's tongue foamed disgustingly over his hands.

Hiccup p-u-l-l-e-d.

The Doomfang p-u-l-l-e-d.

There was only one potato, and both of them wanted it. Both of them NEEDED it. Desperately, Hiccup tried to get a better grip on the potato, slimy and greasy with the yucky bubbly saliva. He wasn't going

to lose the quest, and Fishlegs's

life, NOW, not when they were so close to home, not when the shadow of Berk was so tantalizingly near.

He leaned right back, pulling with a might he never knew he had. But the Doomfang pulled too, and the chances of Hiccup, not more than fifty pounds, winning a tug of war against a Dragon numberless pounds heavier were very tiny indeed.

Not im-POSSIBLE, but, let's face it, im-PROBABLE.

Hiccup did not let go. He would never have let go. He would have stood there all day and all night, if he could have.

But one fork of the Doomfang's tongue unpeeled Hiccup's desperate fingers, one by one, and the other fork gave a horrible squirm, and with a final terrible wrench, the Doomfang's tongue wrested the potato out of Hiccup's hands.

As Hiccup fell backward into the bottom of the boat, he saw with more despair than he had ever felt before in his short adventurous life, the revolting tongue retreat with a flick as quick as a toad catching flies, back into the Doomfang's mouth. The jaws shut over it with awful finality.

The Doomfang swallowed the Potato.

The quest was over.

The Potato was GONE.

The quest was over.

17. THE QUEST IS OVER

Tears pouring down his face, Hiccup watched as the Doomfang threw back its head and screamed as loudly as if it had been shot with a gigantic spear.

It sent a great sheet of freezing blue flame like an uphill waterfall shooting up into the sky. These flames shot so high they hit a small cloud up above, instantly freezing it, and turning it bright blue. And then, just like that, the Doomfang sank slowly beneath the waves, leaving nothing behind but a whirlpool of gigantic ripples, spreading wider and wider.

They spread toward *The Hopeful Puffin*, rocking it violently up and down. They spread wider still, and lapped the shores of Hysteria itself, and carried on down the Wrath of Thor.

Hiccup sat in the bottom of the boat, unable to believe that the Doomfang wouldn't rear up again, and maybe spit out the potato, or give it back in some way. But eventually the ripples got smaller and vanished entirely, and so too did Hiccup's last hope.

This really *was* the end.

The nearest potato was now thousands and

thousands of miles away, in the great country to the west, known as America to those who believe in such a place.

"Issa g-g-g-gone!" whispered Toothless in amazement.

Up on the clifftops, the long line of watching, silent Hysterics began to shout: "THE DOOMFANG IS GONE! THE DOOMFANG IS GONE! HURRAH FOR THE WEIRD LITTLE RED-HAIRED BOY, THE DOOMFANG IS GONE!"

And softly, and silently, snow as blue as Gobber the Belch's nose rained down from the frozen cloud above Hiccup's head.

The blue snow rained down like confetti at a coronation, settling in Hiccup's hair, and on One Eye's white back, and in between Toothless's horns.

"YOU are the Chosen One," said Norbert the Nutjob, still unable to believe it. "YOU have rid us of the Doomfang. YOU have lifted the Curse of Hysteria?"

Hiccup was suddenly furiously angry.

Not with Norbert, but with the gods.

For six long months he had been longing for spring to come, praying to Thor for the ice to melt, and now, just when he and Camicazi had been through so much, and nearly achieved the impossible, just at *precisely* the wrong moment, Thor had made the ice crack and freed the Doomfang.

And this ridiculous blue snow was just the icing on the cake. What was it Snotlout had said?

The snow will turn as blue as Gobber the Belch's nose before YOU become the Chief of the Hairy Hooligan Tribe.

The gods were laughing at him now, playing with him for their sport.

Hiccup shook his fist at the Heavens.

"I don't WANT to be the Chosen One!" he howled at the blue sky above. "I don't WANT to be the Chief of the Hairy Hooligan Tribe! I didn't WANT to lift Norbert's stupid Curse! I wanted to cheat the Curse on *Fishlegs*! All I want is my FRIEND . . ."

The silly blue snow took no notice, and rained down steadily from above.

Hiccup began to cry.

"All I want is my friend . . . ," he sobbed. "Fishlegs trusted me. He thought I would make everything all right . . ." He turned to Norbert in sudden hope.

"Have you got ANOTHER potato?" asked Hiccup.

Norbert the Nutjob shook his head. "My father only brought back ONE of those Vegetables," he said between gritted teeth. "This is what made it so precious . . ."

Norbert the Nutjob shifted his axe uncertainly from hand to hand. The tic in his eye danced a wild fandango.

"I don't know what to do!" shrieked Norbert the Nutjob. "You have shot me in the bottom, stolen my American Vegetable, chewed off my mustaches, fed

Papa to the Squealers, and burned down my Great Hall!"

His shaking hands reached out, almost of their own accord, toward Hiccup's neck . . . and then he stopped himself just in time.

"But on the other hand, it seems incredible, but you HAVE lifted the Curse on Hysteria, and I cannot ignore my father's Prophecy. So THIS TIME, I shall let you go free. But if you ever,

EVER cross my path again, I warn you I will kill you on the spot."

"Don't worry," said Hiccup sadly. "I'm not that keen on seeing YOU again, either. I'm sorry about the Hall, and the mustaches, and the bottom, and . . . I'm sorry about EVERYTHING, really . . . I was just trying to save the life of my friend."

Norbert the Nutjob pulled Hiccup's sword out
of his belt and threw it down with a curse on the floor
of *The Hopeful Puffin*. He then climbed back on board
his sleigh and sped back to Hysteria, a land which
ships could now sail in and out of as freely as they
liked for the first time in fifteen long years, all on
account of Hiccup lifting the Curse, which wasn't the
quest he set out to do in the first place, but, there we
are, these things happen to a Hero-in-Training.

With hearts sorrowing and despairing, Hiccup
and Camicazi set out in *The Hopeful Puffin* toward the
distant little Isle of Berk.

Camicazi took the helm because Hiccup was too depressed.

There was a brisk wind and *The Hopeful Puffin* fairly flew over the waves. They had to dodge the floating icebergs, and if Hiccup had been happier, he could have enjoyed the warmness of the breeze now blowing in their faces, for he had been waiting for this moment for six months.

For six long months they had been trapped in winter, and to Vikings who are used to being surrounded by the never-ending rocking of the sea, this frozen white stillness had been terribly eerie, as if time itself had forgotten to tick and was caught in a Hibernation Coma. There was nothing, no smell, no sound, no movement, just a painted white world that stretched out forever and a cold that made Hiccup's helmet burn against his forehead as if it were made out of fire.

Hiccup had longed and longed for it to end, and now spring HAD come and broken the spell. The sea was alive again and the wind whirling through the marshy grasses carried with it the catcalls and whoops of Dragonese and the lovely fresh smell and taste of salt.

And Hiccup had never been so miserable in his life.

206

"I don't understand," said Camicazi, after they had sailed in silence for half an hour. "*Why* did the Doomfang eat the Vegetable-That-No-One-Dares-Name? *Why* did it suddenly leave the Wrath of Thor when it had been hanging out there for the past fifteen years? *What* just happened?"

Hiccup sighed, raising his head from his chest for a moment. "Well," he said, "I don't KNOW of course, because, how can we know? But my guess is that the DOOMFANG ITSELF HAD VORPENTITIS."

Camicazi's jaw dropped.

"It had all the symptoms," continued Hiccup. "Crazy behavior. Bloodshot eyes. Foaming mouth. A very high temperature. Doomfangs can live to be thousands of years old, so fifteen years is only two minutes in the life of a Doomfang. It would explain how desperate it was, and how ill it looked. And once it had eaten the Potato, it was instantly cured, so it didn't need to hang around anymore. That was it, end of Curse."

"Who is to say that your friend's life is worth more than a Dragon's?" said One Eye, who was taking up most of the deck.

"It's worth more to me," said Hiccup. "Because I didn't know the Doomfang personally."

The temperature was very pleasant, and for the first time in six months Hiccup found he was sweating in his furry overcoat. He took it off, and Toothless landed on his shoulder, and started trying to tuck his head under his wing.

"It's a bit late to go into Hibernation Sleep now, Toothless," said Hiccup, scratching the little dragon affectionately behind his horns. "It's just about to be spring again."

Toothless grunted grumpily.

Hiccup squinted up at the sun. Now that it was out, he could tell the time fairly accurately from the sun's position in the sky. They were at least two hours away from ten in the morning, he reckoned. Not that it mattered what time they got back *now*, of course.

Hiccup's heart was beating fast in anxiety and sadness, and he suddenly realized he could actually HEAR it beating.

Tick tock tick tock tick tock went his heart.

How very peculiar, thought Hiccup.

And then he remembered the funny round metal thing that Camicazi had found lying in the casket next to the potato. He reached into his breast pocket and drew it out.

TICK TOCK TICK TOCK TICK TOCK went the metal thingamajig.

It was a beautifully made, strange little object, slightly smaller than the potato. The front was transparent and hard, like ice, and behind it were all these rune numbers set in different circles, and at least seven arrows, all different colors. When he stared at it for some time he realized that some of them were actually moving, very slowly, but all on their own.

the funny round metal thing

He opened up the back to see if it was a tiny nanodragon making the ticking noise, and found inside nothing but lots of little delicate metal wheels that all seemed to be moving. Perhaps they too had been frozen by the ice, and now that it was warmer again, they had woken up . . .

"WOW," breathed Camicazi, looking over his shoulder. "What is it, do you think?"

"I have no idea," said Hiccup, putting it back in his pocket, where the ticking would be muffled. He would think about it later. "It's some kind of Hysterical invention, I suppose. Those Hysterics are mad as mackerel, but they *are* good inventors."

Please, Thor, please, thought Hiccup to himself, *please let it be all right somehow after all . . .*

It began to rain, and the rain melted the blue snow, and it dripped like tears off the horns on Hiccup's helmet, down into blue puddles on the deck. The American arrow lay, half drowning, on the edge of one of these puddles, and Hiccup picked it up and put it carefully in his arrow case.

Within five minutes, all the snow had gone, and Camicazi, Hiccup, Toothless, and One Eye all looked as if they'd had some kind of weird accident with a lot of blue paint. Their hair, coats, helmets and horns all coated and streaked with the blue of the bluest of blue skies.

Tick tock tick tock tick tock said the metal thingamajig in Hiccup's pocket.

Tick tock tick tock tick tock went Hiccup's heart, hopeful in spite of itself.

Back on Hysteria, steaming through the pouring rain, you could see the bright flame of fire and a column of smoke coming from the Hysterical Great Hall.

Norbert's Papa was finally getting his proper Viking funeral.

18. FISHLEGS

Stoick was waiting for them, in pouring rain, on the
Long Beach.

Stoick was FURIOUS.

He had only just found out that Hiccup had *not*
spent the night at Snotlout's house, and Snotlout had
told him that he had seen Hiccup and Camicazi
sneaking away in a sleigh from the Freya'sday Eve
Celebrations, heading out onto the great sea of ice.

When Stoick demanded why Snotlout had not
told him this earlier, Snotlout could not answer.

Snotlout could hardly give the *real reason*, which
was that he had been rather hoping that Hiccup was
doing something STUPID and DANGEROUS, and
he didn't want Stoick rushing out to save him at the
last minute.

But Stoick the Vast saw the *real reason* in
Snotlout's eyes, and in the delighted way that Snotlout
looked out at the melted ice in the Harbor. Snotlout
was PLEASED that Hiccup could have drowned
somewhere out there in that grey, grim sea.

For the first time, Stoick realized that Snotlout

might not be the best choice of friend for his son Hiccup.

I am afraid that Stoick the Vast gave Snotlout an old-fashioned spanking.

This WAS the Dark Ages.

Stoick then ran to the Long Beach to see if he could see what was going on, and, to his MASSIVE relief, the first thing he clapped eyes on, picking through the icebergs out to sea, was the tattered, round shape of his son's funny little boat, *The Hopeful Puffin.*

"WHAT IN THOR'S NAME DO YOU THINK YOU HAVE BEEN DOING?" roared Stoick the Vast, storming up to them as the nose of *The Hopeful Puffin* landed on the sand. Hiccup, who appeared to have turned an extraordinary blue color, clambered out of the boat and looked his enraged father straight in the eyes.

"I have been to Hysteria, to try and bring back a Potato to save Fishlegs's life," said Hiccup.

Stoick exploded.

"I ABSOLUTELY FORBADE YOU TO DO ANY SUCH THING!" bellowed Stoick the Vast. "HOW DARE YOU DISOBEY ME, YOUR CHIEF, AND RISK YOUR LIVES LOOKING FOR A

VEGETABLE THAT NEVER EXISTED, ON A
WILD-GOOSE CHASE FOR NOTHING —"

Tears poured down Hiccup's face. "The potato
DOES exist," he interrupted his father, "it DOES
exist, because we stole it, and Norbert the Nutjob
nearly chopped our heads off, but you are right, it
WAS all for nothing, because the Doomfang ate it
and now Fishlegs is going to DIE."

Stoick the Vast's anger could not last in the face
of the utter hopeless misery in his son's eyes. His fury
melted away, like the snow dissolving into rain all
around them on the beach. He patted his son
awkwardly on the shoulder.

"Now, now, son," he said uncertainly. "*Of course*
Fisheggs isn't going to die . . ."

Hiccup pushed his father out of the way and
stumbled over the sand to Old Wrinkly's house,
followed by Stoick the Vast, Camicazi, Toothless, and
One Eye. He flung open the door without knocking.

Old Wrinkly was standing in the middle of the
room, poking the fire with a metal stick.

For a moment, Hiccup couldn't see Fishlegs, and
then he realized Fishlegs was on the bed. He was lying
completely still, his glasses off, white as a corpse.

Hiccup's heart stopped.

And then to Hiccup's unspeakable relief, Fishlegs sat up and put his glasses on.

He was still alive, then.

Stoick the Vast, Camicazi, Toothless, and One Eye the Saber-Toothed Driver filed into the room after Hiccup.

"WELL?" roared Stoick the Vast. "IS FISHEGGS DYING, OR IS HE NOT?"

Old Wrinkly looked very embarrassed. He shifted guiltily from foot to foot. "Ah, yes, Stoick, I'm so glad you brought that up . . . yes, the thing is, I'm not sure that Fishlegs is dying after all . . ."

"WHADDYAMEAN, NOT DYING?" yelled Stoick the Vast.

"I'm afraid my diagnosis wasn't completely correct." Old Wrinkly giggled nervously. "Soothsaying from the fire is very complicated. . . . I won't go into the details, but take it from me, it's *tricky* . . . and, what with one thing or another, it turns out that Fishlegs didn't have Vorpentitis after all. It was just a bad cold that set off his Berserk tendencies. I nursed him back to health with lots of bed rest and lemon-in-honey."

Fishlegs stood up, slightly wobbly, and gave Stoick the Vast a big smile.

"I'm *fine!*" said Fishlegs happily, throwing wide his arms.

Hiccup couldn't believe it.

It was going to be all right after all.

"HE'S ALIVE!" cried Hiccup joyously, over the moon at this uncomplicated happy ending, and he rushed over to hug his friend.

Toothless gave
Fishlegs a lick on the ear,
which was a big compliment from
Toothless. One Eye drawled, "Well,
well, that was all worth it, wasn't it?" and
Camicazi did a couple of celebratory cartwheels.

But Stoick wasn't going to take this lying down.

"DO YOU MEAN TO TELL ME," roared
Stoick the Vast at Old Wrinkly, "THAT ALL
BECAUSE OF YOUR LOUSY SOOTHSAYING
MY SON HICCUP HAS GONE ALL THE WAY
TO HYSTERIA AND NEARLY GOT HIS
HEAD CHOPPED OFF BY NORBERT THE
NUTJOB AND FACED THE DOOMFANG
ALL FOR NOTHING??????"

"Well, not for *nothing*, Stoick," explained
Old Wrinkly. "If you'll just listen a moment, I'll
explain. Soothsaying is a very tricky business and
when I looked in the fire —"

"*Did* Fisheggs have Vorpentitis, or did he
not?" interrupted Stoick.

"No, he didn't," admitted Old Wrinkly.

"THEN THE QUEST WAS COMPLETELY UNNECESSARY!" roared Stoick.

"Don't give Old Wrinkly a hard time, Father," said Hiccup. "Why waste time getting angry when all's well that ends well . . ."

Hiccup started to laugh, but something in the middle of the laugh went wrong when Hiccup's left arm suddenly went dead.

Hiccup looked down at his arm in surprise.

"I can't feel my arm," said Hiccup.

And then the other arm went dead.

Hiccup had been feeling rather hot all day, but he suddenly felt as if he were burning alive. Sweat poured down his face, and great clouds of steam rose up off his shoulders and chest.

218

And Hiccup Horrendous Haddock
the Third's entire body went rigid as a statue,
his eyes staring and bloodshot, and he fell down lifeless
on the very bed Fishlegs had been lying on just two
minutes before.

19. THE FINAL CHAPTER

Sometimes it is not until the Final Chapter that you realize what a quest has REALLY been about all along.

Stoick's face turned from red anger to pure white terror.

"The Doomfang . . . ," whispered Stoick the Vast in agony, rushing to hold his stiff son in his arms. "By Woden and Freya and Hairy Knuckled Thor, he *did* get touched by the frozen flames of the Doomfang . . . and all for a stupid useless quest for NOTHING . . ."

Enormous, hairy Stoick the Vast burst into tears.

"Oh for Thor's sake, Stoick," cried Old Wrinkly, bossily pushing Stoick out of the way. "Will you just SHUT UP and listen to me? I'm really not *that* bad a soothsayer. This has nothing to do with the Doomfang." He took Hiccup's pulse, and looked under his eyelids, and tapped his chest, which had turned as wooden as a tree trunk. "*This* is VORPENTITIS."

Stoick reeled back. "And what does that mean?" he whispered through white lips.

"It means," said Old Wrinkly, "that one little weirdo looks very like another when you're soothsaying in a fire, and it was HICCUP who was bitten by the Vorpent, and not Fishlegs. So HICCUP has Vorpentitis. And that means that since it is now . . ."

(At this point Old Wrinkly reached into Hiccup's breast pocket, hoping to draw out the potato, and in fact drew out the ticking metal thingamajig. He looked at the numbers on it and nodded his head.)

". . . oooh *exactly* five to ten in the morning on Freya'sday Friday!" continued Old Wrinkly, laying the metal thingamajig carefully on the bed beside Hiccup, "your son, Hiccup, who has Vorpentitis, has five minutes to live."

Old Wrinkly chuckled. This didn't seem to be worrying him much.

"Which wouldn't give a great deal of time for us to find an antidote. But luckily," said Old Wrinkly, in the spirit of a conjuror, "*luckily*, on your son's so-called stupid useless quest for NOTHING, he has brought back the antidote with him ALREADY. Camicazi, where is the potato? It doesn't seem to be here in Hiccup's pocket. . . . Have *you* got it?"

Camicazi was as white as One Eye's back. She shook her head numbly. "No . . . potato," she gasped.

Old Wrinkly's mouth fell open, appalled.

221

"NO POTATO?" shrieked Old Wrinkly. "WHAT DO YOU MEAN, **NO POTATO?** YOU MUST HAVE THE POTATO!!!"

Camicazi shook her head again. "No potato," she whispered.

"But I was so sure," whispered Old Wrinkly. "I was so *sure* you would bring back the potato. . . . This is the last time I believe a single word those beastly fires say. . . . They told me **DEFINITELY** that you would get it . . ."

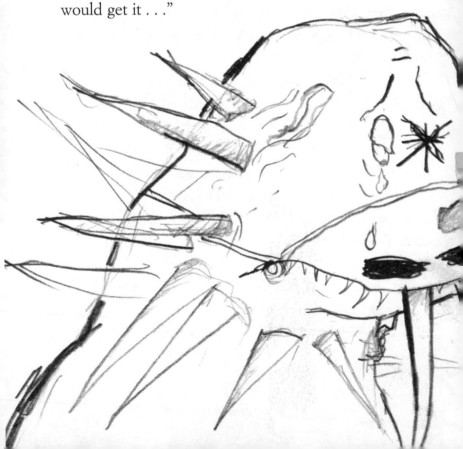

"Oh, we *got* it all right," mumbled Camicazi miserably. "It was just that the Doomfang ATE it."

"Oh, my goodness," gulped Old Wrinkly.

NO POTATO.

Suddenly Old Wrinkly looked every second of his ninety-three years. His whole body crumpled up like an old brown leaf.

Little did Hiccup know, when he was crying on the boat for his friend Fishlegs, that he should have been crying for himself.

For it was indeed HICCUP who had been stung all those many months ago, escaping from the Fortress of Sinister.

And it was Hiccup who was now moments away from the death he feared for his friend Fishlegs.

"WHAT CAN I DO?" roared Stoick the Vast. "There must be other cures? Other medicines?"

Old Wrinkly shook his head. "The potato is the only cure for Vorpentitis."

"I'LL BRING BACK THE POTATO!" cried Stoick the Vast, drawing his sword, a Man of Action to the last. "JUST TELL ME WHERE TO GO AND HOW LONG I'VE GOT!"

"Well," said Old Wrinkly sadly, "the nearest potato is now roughly three and a half thousand miles away on the distant shores of the country known as America to those who may believe in it. And you have . . ." — Old Wrinkly checked the clock sitting next to Hiccup's bed — ". . . exactly THREE minutes to find it."

Even Stoick seemed to feel that perhaps this might be a problem.

He strode around the room, tearing at his beard.

Old Wrinkly, Camicazi, and One Eye sat at Hiccup's bedside.

One Eye didn't seem as happy as he might have been two days ago at the thought of one less Human in the world.

A big tear rolled out of his one eye and down his Saber-Tooth and plopped onto the ground.

Hiccup was stiff as a board, and his body was now red, and boiling hot. Toothless licked his poor red face, to try to cool it down.

"THE DOOMFANG!" cried Stoick the Vast. "I COULD TRACK DOWN THE DOOMFANG AND WRESTLE THE POTATO FROM HIM!"

"You're going to find the Doomfang in the vast and trackless wastes of an immense and fathomless Ocean," said Old Wrinkly wearily, checking the time again on the clock, "in TWO minutes?"

"Face it, Stoick," whispered Old Wrinkly. "What you're talking about is not just im-PROBABLE . . . it's im-POSSIBLE . . ."

Fishlegs had drawn back into the shadows, and he was watching his friend's face.

Hiccup was trying to say something, but his frozen, burning mouth made it difficult for him to say the words.

In fact he looked very like the Doomfang, when he was trying to speak to Hiccup out on the Sullen Sea.

"Ooot me . . . ," mumbled Hiccup desperately. "OOOOOT ME!" and he tried to point, but his arms were as stiff as if they were made out of wood.

Old Wrinkly patted his hand, and bathed his forehead with water. Stoick's shoulders heaved with sobs.

"OOOOT ME!" cried poor Hiccup again.

Fishlegs tried to follow where his friend's eyes were looking, and it seemed like they were staring at the table by the door.

On that table lay Hiccup's furry coat and his helmet, bow, and arrows that he had thrown there when he first came in the room.

"One minute left," whispered Old Wrinkly.

"OOOOOOOOOOT ME!" repeated Hiccup desperately.

Sometimes it is only a True Friend who knows what we mean when we try to speak.

Somebody who has spent a lot of time with us, and listens carefully to what we are trying to say, and tries to understand.

Fishlegs understood.

He didn't know *why* he was supposed to do what he was about to do, but he trusted Hiccup, who always seemed to know the right thing to do.

Fishlegs picked up Hiccup's bow.

Out of the arrow case he drew an arrow, a singularly beautiful arrow, decorated with feathers from birds Fishlegs had never seen before.

Fishlegs fitted the arrow to the bow, and pointed the bow toward Hiccup.

Stoick looked up from his sobbing, in amazement. Here was his son, moments away from dying, and that weird fish-faced friend of his appeared to be about to SHOOT him. TYPICAL. What a nutcase.

"O-O-O-!" cried Stoick. "DON'T SHOOT!"

Stoick threw his vast bulk across the room in an attempt to shield his son from the arrow.

Of course, he was trying to protect Hiccup's heart and chest. He didn't realize what an appalling shot Fishlegs was, so he jumped far too high.

Fishlegs let the arrow go, and it soared in a wobbly unsteady arc, finally landing in Hiccup's right big toe, piercing through his wet boots, and into the skin.

It was a bit of a miracle it hit Hiccup at all. In fact, it may just be the only time Fishlegs has EVER hit something he was actually *aiming* at.

The arrow that pierced the skin of Hiccup's big toe at ten o'clock on the morning of Freya'sday Friday was the same arrow that had been soaking for the last fifteen years in the magical juices of THE POTATO.

Over the past decade and a half, those juices had concentrated on the surface of the metal, and the antidote now made its way into Hiccup's bloodstream, taking its cooling, healing work up every little vein, down every little artery, into every little corner of Hiccup's poor, rigid, boiling little body.

In front of their eyes, Hiccup's stiff arms softened. His chest rose and fell. The breath blew out of his nostrils, and his eyes opened.

"Hello, Father," said Hiccup.

This was just too much for Stoick. He fainted dead away, on the spot, all six foot seven and three-feet round of him, and it took a great deal more trouble to revive HIM.

He was out cold, and Old Wrinkly slapped him, and Hiccup shook him, and Camicazi tickled his feet, and eventually it was Fishlegs who ran out and filled an enormous bucket full of snow, and threw it right in Stoick's face. *That* brought him to his senses, and Stoick sat bolt upright, spluttering and spitting snow out of his beard.

"You're ALIVE!" he shouted joyfully, and he hugged his son so hard Hiccup thought his ribs might crack. "By the Bristly Beard and Thunderous Thighs of Great Goddess Freya, you're ALIVE!"

"He *is* alive," said Old Wrinkly pointedly, "and I think some apologies are in order."

Stoick's brows lowered. However relieved and

happy he is, a Great Chieftain used to absolute power
does not like to apologize, but after a short struggle,
Stoick swallowed his pride.

"You are right," said Stoick. "I have been
thoroughly wrong, and I am sorry. Old Wrinkly, you are
not the most pathetic soothsayer in the uncivilized
world, and I am sorry I ever said you were. Hiccup,
you were *right* to go on the quest for the Frozen Potato
to try and save the life of your odd little friend."

Stoick turned to Fishlegs.

"And most of all, FISHEGGS," he boomed solemnly, "I have misjudged YOU."

Fishlegs blushed. "No, no," he stammered.

"Yes," said Stoick, holding up a hairy hand. "I have. A Chief has to be big enough to admit it when he is wrong. You *are* a little weirdo, it is true, but you are a LOYAL little weirdo, and one day when my son is Chief I have a feeling he will need some loyal people about him."

Meanwhile, Toothless, who really couldn't stand all this soppy hugging and apologizing, flapped away to find a nice warm spot by the fire.

"Hiccup," Toothless called out sleepily, when he had found himself a particularly cozy position, "issa anyone else gonna d-d-die inna next f-f-five minutes?"

Hiccup laughed, and he asked Old Wrinkly.

"No," said Old Wrinkly solemnly. "I have examined the fire very carefully, and I can say, absolutely DEFINITELY, that NOBODY is going to die in the next five minutes. However, Gobber the Belch, I'm afraid, will catch Fishlegs's cold, and it's a nasty one."

"OK then," yawned Toothless. "Iffa no one need T-t-toothless, Toothless go back to sleep."

So just when the Inner Isles were waking up from the coldest, longest winter in a hundred years, when the snow was melting, when all the other hunting dragons were opening their eyes underground preparing to burrow upward, and spring was eventually deciding it was time to arrive, just at *this* moment, Toothless FINALLY relaxed and went back into Hibernation Sleep.

One Eye settled down next to him, snoring like a dinosaur with sinus problems.

Old Wrinkly began to explain to Stoick some of the finer points of soothsaying.

And Hiccup and his good friends Fishlegs and Camicazi wandered outside to spend the rest of the day not doing very much at all — my favorite kind of day.

As for Gobber the Belch, why Gobber the Belch woke up with a throbbing head and a sore throat and a nose that ran like a great green river.

So it appears that Vikings DO catch colds after all . . .

Vikings don't get sick... flu is for softies... plagues are for girlies...

A-A-A-CHOO!

236

EPILOGUE BY HICCUP HORRENDOUS HADDOCK THE THIRD, THE LAST OF THE GREAT VIKING HEROES

I guessed, but never knew for *sure*, what had happened in that strange frozen moment in my childhood, when the Doomfang stole my potato.

But many years later, when I was a tall young man in command of my first ship and we were just returning home from some wild and dangerous adventure, we suddenly realized that we were being *followed* by something. For days and days it followed us, always staying at the same distance behind the boat. I spent hours up the mast watching the black pinprick on the horizon and trying to work out what it was, whale or shark or dragon monster, friend or foe, with some nagging feeling at the back of my mind that this was something I recognized from somewhere in my past.

It wasn't until we entered the Sullen Sea that the creature came right up close. It was immediately clear from its glossy dark color that it was a Doomfang. It didn't attack us, as I had been secretly dreading, but began to play with the boat, swimming alongside, diving underneath and coming up the other side, getting nearer and nearer with each circle that it made.

This is common enough behavior in dolphins, and even in humpback whales, who are fascinated by boats, and will play like this for hours. But it is hugely unusual in a Doomfang. Doomfangs normally have the same attitude toward humans that *we* have toward insects: they loftily ignore us.

But this Doomfang was different. Even though it was clearly a fully grown animal, at least five times as long and as big as our ship, it played with us like a child, swimming around and around the boat, until finally the great creature gave a mighty thrash with its tail and soared out of the water, spreading wide its wings. It jumped right over the ship, just clearing the mast.

My Warriors gasped in awe and fear and amazement and wonder, as the great long body blocked out the sun, and I gasped too, for I recognized the animal at last. This was *my* Doomfang, not slain, not dead, not gone away, but in the very pink of health, and it seemed rather pleased with itself, and with me.

For when it entered the water on the other side,

the great Doomfang tucked its legs up neatly and entered the water at exactly the right angle, so that it would not cause a single ripple to rock our little boat. And when the creature swam alongside, so close now that we could reach out and touch its glistening raven black sides, it rolled onto its back and moved its wing almost like it was waving, and its terrible mouth seemed to be grinning at me.

That very same Doomfang has followed my boat ever after, not like a Doom or a Curse, but more like a guardian angel.

I have lost count of the times when I have been out at sea in the most dreadful peril (for we Vikings lead dangerous and exciting lives) and just at the moment when all hope is lost, the Doomfang has appeared.

That Doomfang has steered my boat through the Great Storm that drowned a thousand ships in the Restless West Sea; it has rescued me from shipwreck on Cannibal Isle; it has fought great Monsters that had my ship wrapped around with their squids' tentacles like a cat's cradle.

It has returned the favor I once did it of saving its life in a cold, cold world, a hundred times over.

It is following me still, even though I don't need rescuing so much now I am old and slow as a great sea turtle, and my hair is as white as a Semi-Spotted Snowpecker.

You *can* Cheat a Dragon's Curse.

You do not have to accept the hand that Fate has dealt you.

Look at *me*, the skinniest, most unlikely Viking *ever*, now known as this great Hero all around the world. Again and again, I have the same dream. Norbert the Nutjob has thrown the axe high, high into the air, it is turning around and around, and the black side is going to plunge into the ground first. . . . Bad Luck will follow and the Tribe will be DOOMED. Again and again I make the same leap, I dodge the bright and black murderous blades, I catch the axe before it lands, I make my own luck.

If none of this had happened, the potato would still be stuck frozen on Hysteria, of no use to anybody. Instead of which, I buried the arrow which saved my life in some muddy ground behind my house, and, miracle of miracles! A single seed must have been sticking to the metal!

For some time later, in the springtime, I noticed

a strange green plant in that particular spot, and I dug the arrow up again. A new potato, larger than the one I lost, had grown right around the arrow's point. From that new potato, I grew *more* potatoes, and now there are potatoes growing all over Berk and the whole of the Barbaric Archipelago, and not a SINGLE PERSON or dragon has died a terrible death from Vorpent stings EVER SINCE.

(The potatoes are also rather delicious when they are cooked, either mashed or just plain with a little dollop of melted butter.)

But more important still, if I had never gone on the quest for the Frozen Potato, I would never have saved the life of my good friend Fishlegs, who, although *some* people thought of him as a little weirdo, was the best and truest friend a Viking ever —

HANG ON A SECOND.

You see how confusing all of this is.

I didn't save the life of my good friend Fishlegs, after all, did I? Because Fishlegs was never ill in the first place.

I saved myself.

What Happens Next?

Will Norbert the Nutjob set out on a Quest to go back to America? And, indeed, does this land they call America **really** exist, and is the world **really** a circle that has no end?

And what has happened to **Alvin the Treacherous**, Hiccup's archenemy, who we rather hoped had been killed when he dropped from a hot-air balloon into a sea boiling with ravenous Sharkworms? I can't think **how** he might have gotten out of **that** tricky situation . . .

But I have a nasty feeling in the pit of my stomach that Hiccup hasn't seen the last of these two mad, wicked, and dangerous villains, both of whom have sworn to kill him . . .

Watch out for the next volume of Hiccup's memoirs . . .